CASSIDY'S
GIRL

CASSIDY'S GIRL

DAVID GOODIS

Introduction by Geoffrey O'Brien

Black Lizard Books
Berkeley • 1987

Copyright © 1951 by Fawcett Publications, Inc. Copyright
© renewed 1979 by The Estate of David Goodis. Black Lizard
Books edition published 1987. All rights reserved. For information
contact: Black Lizard Books, 833 Bancroft Way, Berkeley, CA
94710. Black Lizard Books are distributed by Creative Arts Book
Company.

Introduction copyright © 1987 by Geoffrey O'Brien.

Composition by QuadraType.

ISBN 0-88739-027-7.
Library of Congress Catalog Card No. 86-70426

Manufactured in the United States of America

Introduction

David Goodis (1917-1967) has always been the mystery man of hardboiled fiction. Even his most ardent (mostly French) admirers had little but his name and dates to go on— while at the same time the savage content of his novels of low life and petty crime left plenty of room for imagination. Goodis was one of the most distinctive writers of paperback originals: a single-page of his work is instantly recognizable, as much for its prose style as for its characteristic obsessions. He wrote of winos and barroom piano players and small-time thieves in a vein of tortured lyricism all his own, whose very excesses seemed uniquely appropriate to the subject matter. As his titles announce—*Street of the Lost*, *Street of No Return*, *The Wounded and the Slain*, *Down There*—he was a poet of the losers, transforming swift cut-rate melodramas into traumatic visions of failed lives.

His own life, long hidden, has become a little clearer thanks to the French writer Philippe Garnier, whose recent biography of Goodis[1] (as yet untranslated) dredges up the secret corners of a life spent very much out of the public eye. As far as the world at large was concerned, Goodis pretty much fell through the cracks, and one's growing impression is that he wanted it that way. His career was not so much the *Retreat from Oblivion* that his first novel proclaimed as it was a voluntary and secretive descent into oblivion.

Yet clearly he was not without ambition. Born in Philadelphia, of a Jewish family struggling through the Depression on the fringes of the middle class, he apparently thought of himself as a writer from an early age. The first book appeared in 1938, the same year he graduated from Temple

---

[1]*Goodis: la vie en noir et blanc.* By Philippe Garnier. Editions du Seuil, 1984.

University—although going by the reviews it was no triumph: "The opening sentence of *Retreat from Oblivion* is as follows: 'After a while it gets so bad that you want to stop the whole business.' It refers to Herb's state of mind, but it's not an inaccurate summary of what one is inclined to say about David Goodis' novel." Rejected as a serious novelist, Goodis turned to the pulps, where he churned out endless aviation stories for magazines like *Battle Birds* and *Daredevil Aces*, and to radio, where he scripted *Hap Harrigan of the Airwaves*. His pulp writing, to judge by an early novella like "Red Wings for the Doomed," had little individuality; however, the experience unquestionably fostered the narrative craft which keeps his novels from dissolving into a morass of psychological analysis.

By 1946 Goodis was ready with another novel—*Dark Passage*—and this made considerably more of a splash. It remains one of his best-known books—the only one, in fact, that really made it into the mainstream. Today its appeal derives less from its none too believable plot (it was one of the early new-face-through-plastic-surgery stories) than from the author's obviously intense identification with his persecuted hero and from the jazzlike pulse of the prose. (Hero and heroine are drawn together in part by their taste for Count Basie.) With the sale of serial rights to the *Saturday Evening Post* and movie rights to Warner Brothers, Goodis had abruptly arrived. *Dark Passage* became a Bogart-Bacall vehicle and Goodis went on the Warners payroll as a staff writer.

He was barely 30, but his career had already peaked. *Dark Passage* was followed by another hardcover novel, *Behold This Woman*, a frequently ludicrous exercise in the *Leave Her to Heaven* "wicked woman" genre. The book is indispensable for its glimpses of Goodis' erotic obsessions, but it cannot have done much for his reputation as a writer. As for the screenwriting stint, all that came of it was an undistinguished remake of *The Letter* (Vincent Sherman's *The Unfaithful*) and an unproduced treatment which became his last hardcover novel (*Of Missing Persons*). He came close to interesting producer Jerry Wald in his concept for an epic film on "the entrance of our civilization into the atomic era": this was as grandiose a notion as Goodis was to be involved with. Henceforth his work would seek lower levels—much lower.

He had published one other novel during the Hollywood years, *Nightfall* (1947), a moderately successful thriller which in retrospect seems an almost perfect book, spare, balanced, and inexplicably moving. (The same might be said of the wonderful film Jacques Tourneur made of it a decade later.) The plot line—another innocent man on the run—could not be more routine. But in *Nightfall* Goodis creates an atmosphere where everything is symbolic—the oppressive heat of a summer night, a metal box of watercolors that crashes to the floor, the winding staircase where words of betrayal are overheard, the mountains toward which the hero flees—and at the same time densely literal.

Of Missing Persons, the banal police procedural salvaged from Warner Brothers, turned out to be his farewell to cloth covers. Goodis had no flair for writing about policemen or other authority figures. Only by identifying with criminals, derelicts, outcasts of some sort, could he come alive as a writer. His movie career was over by now too; indeed, his whole life evidently went into reverse gear. In 1950 he went back to Philadelphia (it isn't clear whether he quit Warners or was let go) and to his family: he would live with his parents until their deaths, shortly before his own. At this point he settled into ten years of paperback originals, mostly for Gold Medal books. There is no evidence that he had high artistic goals in mind. More likely he chose a kind of fiction which would support him while guaranteeing a cloak of anonymity. He doesn't seem to have wanted any sort of fame.

Garnier's account leaves no doubt as to Goodis' profound eccentricity. During the Hollywood years, for instance, he lived in the Los Angeles home of a lawyer friend, Allen Norkin, renting not a room but a tiny uncomfortable sofa for $4 a week—at a time when, as a movie writer, he could have lived well. Goodis apparently refused to spend money on almost anything: not out of miserliness but from a sheer perversity which also led him to drive the same battered Chrysler convertible virtually his whole adult life, a car so miserable that his friends refused to be seen in it. His clothing, as Norkin recounts, was equally grotesque: "He wore my old suits, and when they were really too worn out, he had them dyed blue. Finally his whole wardrobe was blue. . . . One day he invited me to eat at the Warner commissary. Dan Duryea was there, and Dave was wearing one of my white suits—which was all yellowed and stained. Duryea asked him where he had dug up the suit, and David replied coldly that he had bought it at Gordon's, one of the best tailors in Philadelphia. And when Duryea remarked that the suit wasn't even ironed, David gave him a pitying glance and explained that that was how it was meant to be worn. He also had an old bathrobe of mine. He went out at night in it. When he wore it he pretended to be a White Russian, an exiled prince of the blood." Goodis would borrow labels from his friends' finest clothes and laboriously sew them into his own wretched hand-me-downs, all for the peculiar pleasure of stopping people short when they criticized his clothing.

He also had a penchant for bizarre practical jokes like stuffing the red cellophane strips from Lucky Strike packs up his nostril, in order to simulate a nosebleed in the midst of a posh restaurant; or screaming with pain while pretending to be caught in a revolving door; or rolling down the steps of a movie theater as if the victim of an accident. But even more puzzling to Goodis' circle (which consisted mostly of old friends from Philadelphia) was his night life. According to what he told his friends, he preferred to spend his time in the sleaziest bars and nightclubs in the black ghettoes of Los Angeles and Philadelphia, in search of the most grossly obese women he could find. This obsession will ring a bell with readers of his novels, in which fat women play a major and often sinister role—nor are we too surprised to learn that what Goodis really craved from these women was extreme verbal abuse. In fact one is inclined to guess—given the overt masochism which continually surfaces in his books—that he went in for even harsher forms of abuse: but that is pure surmise. He was a man of fantasies, of masquerades. His night life—even the whole squalid world of his books—may have sprung largely from his imagination. Garnier even claims—astonishingly, considering the alcoholism of nearly all

Goodis' protagonists—that the novelist himself was not a drinker. On the other hand Knox Burger, once Goodis' editor at Gold Medal, describes him as "a strange guy. He lived with his mother, in his forties, and would go off on these wild tears."

With the move to paperback originals, the style and content of his books changed radically. As if mirroring the failure of Goodis' higher-toned literary ambitions, the novels turned decisively toward the lower depths. From here on he would be the chronicler of skid row, and specifically of the man fallen from his social class: the disgraced airline pilot (*Cassidy's Girl*), the artist turned art appraiser for a gang of burglars (*Black Friday*), the famous crooner turned streetcorner bum (*Street of No Return*), the concert performer turned barroom piano player (*Down There*). In this fashion David Goodis, great literary artist turned streetcorner hack writer, could tell his own story and ply his trade at the same time.

Cassidy's Girl (1951) was the first and, judging from the number of reprints, the most popular of his paperbacks. It contains most of the elements of the later novels: an environment of grinding poverty, a sensitive but inarticulate male protagonist largely unaware of his self-destructive tendencies, and two women who divide his energies, with melodramatic consequences—one of them a frail ghostly alcoholic haunted by unrealizable dreams (let us call her Type A), the other a fat, rough-tongued, hard-drinking (and hard-fighting) woman who will stop at nothing to keep the hero to herself (Type B). There are many recurring relationships in Goodis' novels, but this polarity between two images of woman is always central; and the hero, caught up by his own lack of self-knowledge, is usually destroyed by it. He sees Type A as his true love, his only hope for happiness, from whom he is kept apart by Type B, who holds him in bondage through marriage, blackmail, or even the threat of physical force. What he can never admit is that he himself in some way sets up the no-win situation, and that indeed it is the Type B woman, that obese and muscular caricature of female dominance, that he really desires. Aside from establishing this tumultuous triad,

Cassidy's Girl is notable for the schematic cruelty with which Goodis loads the dice against the hapless Cassidy. Disaster hangs around the fallen airline pilot like a magnetic, almost seductive aura.

The novels which followed—one or two a year for the next decade—were by no means all on the same level. *Street of the Lost* (1952), for instance, proves the most ham-handed of the Gold Medal books, emphasizing the prolonged fistfights which were a Goodis sideline—he evidently had at least a fan's knowledge of boxing, and so his accounts have a somewhat pedantic precision—and the even more prolonged drinking bouts which began to dominate his fiction. The next title, *Of Tender Sin* (1952), extending the alcoholic theme, resembles a poor man's *Lost Weekend:* Al Darby (one of Goodis' occasional white-collar heroes), tormented by the impotence which is destroying his marriage, embarks on an epic binge, revisiting the impoverished scenes of his youth, playing out a paranoid jealous fantasy almost to the point of committing murder, receiving wisdom from an old Negro on skid row (one of many philosophical bums to follow), and ultimately reawaking the repressed memory of an incestuous episode which is supposed to be the root of his troubles. Many of Goodis' novels follow a similar psychoanalytic pattern; the thrust of his books is usually toward release, redemption, resolution of conflict, and there are even some theoretically "happy" endings; but whatever salvation Goodis as author may cook up for his characters, it never adds up to more than literary wishful thinking. The despair does not go away.

The Burglar (1953) was the first of three books that Goodis wrote for Lion, the enterprising paperback house which published the bulk of Jim Thompson's works. These were sharper-edged than the Gold Medal novels, with fewer uncontrolled descents into self-pity and (in two cases out of three) with more emphasis on crime. *The Burglar* stands out for its evocation of a Romantic death-wish in the context of low-grade crooks coming unraveled in the wake of a bungled break-in. The prose style is notable as well: Goodis seems to have really worked on this one, piling on little flourishes of syncopation that remind us how musical his ear could sometimes be. If Jack Kerouac had written crime novels they might have sounded a bit like this. *The Burglar* was later filmed by Paul Wendkos, a close friend who filmed on location in Philadelphia and hired Goodis himself to write the screenplay. It's in many ways an odd movie—starting with the pairing of Dan Duryea and Jayne Mansfield as the doomed lovers—but a true evocation of Goodis' universe.

In its back cover blurb for *The Burglar*, Lion proclaimed: "Twenty years ago it was HAMMETT . . . for the first time telling the crime story with raw and savage truth . . . Ten years ago it was CHANDLER . . . taking the realism one step further—into the nightmare world of a murderer's mind . . . Today it is DAVID GOODIS . . . pushing the crime novel forward into a new dimension—probing into the heart of the thief and the killer." Whatever the accuracy of this as literary history, it pinpoints Goodis' originality quite well. The strength of his novels is the way his characters' emotions color every sentence, every line of dialogue, every fragment of physical description. It wouldn't be hard to imagine one of his books transformed into an opera—*Cassidy's Girl*, perhaps, as a swelling exercise in *verismo*. While at his worst Goodis merely overwrites, at his best he endows his icy streets and wretched shanties with expressionistic intensity.

The central law of Goodis' fiction is that happiness is forbidden. All true love remains unconsummated; all petty criminals (a breed with whom the author closely identifies) are caught ignominiously; all proud old men are humiliated; all virgins are molested. The sentimental lyricism of Goodis' prose masks a savage perception of life. In *The Moon in the Gutter* (1953), a dockworker's sister is raped; she slits her throat with a razor in a garbage-strewn alleyway. Later in the book, a slumming socialite trying to seduce the dockworker drives him over to the harbor, saying "It's really magnificent." He replies with a nauseating description of the smell and texture of bilgewater, and when she recoils adds: "I'm only trying to give you the full picture. You come down to see the dirt, I'm showing you the dirt." In a memorably overblown final monologue, he indicts the moon shining above the gutter for his sister's death.

Goodis published three novels in 1954, two of them among his best. Gold Medal's *Street of No Return* almost ranks as an epic: a wino's odyssey from nowhere to nowhere. Three bums stand on a corner trying to figure out how to get a drink. One of them wanders off and comes back 175 pages later, a bottle under his coat, having relived his entire life: his career as a pop singer shattered by an obsessive love for a prostitute, his torture by racketeers and his beating at the hands of the police, his final turn as a reluctant hero foiling a conspiracy to foment a race riot— only to find that all he really wants to do is go back to the corner. Here Goodis came closest to acknowledging that his heroes' tragic destinies were largely self-created. His battered protagonist finally admits to himself: "You've played a losing game and actually enjoyed the idea of losing, almost like them freaks who get their kicks when they're banged around. . . . You're in that same bracket, buddy. You're one of them less-than-nothings who like the taste of being hurt." He moves inevitably toward the numbed retreat of the book's final sentence: "They sat there passing the bottle around, and there was nothing that could bother them, nothing at all."

In a similar spirit, the artist hero of *Black Friday*, having witnessed the violent collapse of the gang of burglars he had joined and the self-sacrificing death of the pale girl he loved, walks off into the night: "He had no idea where he was going and he didn't care." A more elaborate variation on the themes of *The Burglar*, *Black Friday* shows Goodis at a peak of tonal control. His sense of the criminal band as a world apart, with its own hermetic codes of respect and kinship, informs every action in the book from first to last. Outside the law there is no freedom, only a stifling web of compulsions and obligations.

A key to all this inner turmoil can be found in *The Blonde on the Street Corner*, a period piece set in the 1930s and which has all the earmarks of an autobiographical novel. (Apparently it has some connection with his unfilmed scenario about the atomic era.) The young hero, whose family struggles, like Goodis', with the adversities of the Depression, is an aspiring songwriter still buoyed by the optimism of youth. The novel is essentially the story of how his hopes are nipped in the bud as he yields to the aggressive advances of the blonde of the title, a violent, alcoholic older woman who brings him face to face with his real sexual nature. This work stands alone in the Goodis *oeuvre*, and is by the way another example of Lion Books' remarkable openness to the offbeat.

The remaining books can be dealt with more cursorily. *The Wounded and the Slain* (1955) offers us another white-collar drunk, on vacation in Jamaica with his frigid wife and doing his best to get himself killed in barroom brawls. This is Goodis' most thorough dissection of alcoholism, but the book rapidly loses credibility as the hero becomes accidentally involved with the Kingston underworld and ends by triumphing over his problems in a clumsily arranged denouement. Far more successful is *Down There* (1956), best known as the source of Francois Truffaut's *Shoot the Piano Player*. Here Goodis blends two of his favorite themes—the artist on the skids and the criminal gang as surrogate family (in this case the gang *is* a family)—to produce his last really satisfying novel. (*Down There* might be seen as the last panel of a triptych also encompassing *The Burglar* and *Black Friday*.)

The next book, *Fire in the Flesh* (1957), purveys the unlikely tale of a pyromaniac who discovers that the only way he can control his impulses is to immerse himself in cheap wine. In a final catharsis he realizes the roots of his obsession and is cured. *Night Squad* (1961), another minor effort, concerns a crooked cop turned alcoholic who likewise finds redemption at the eleventh hour. Goodis' last novel, the posthumously published *Somebody's Done For* (1967), amounts to a pot-pourri of his major preoccupations—the two women, the gang as family, alcoholism, impotence, incest—played out on a barren strip of New Jersey shoreline. These final works, presumably reflecting the author's state of mind, are suffused with a depression that creeps into the rhythm of the sentences.

From about midway in his career Goodis shows every

sign of having reached a personal impasse. The obsessions laid bare in his novels begin to repeat themselves rather than developing creatively. But taken as a whole his writing represents an astonishing example of self-revelation in the context of genre fiction. Anyone who spends some time with his books learns to identify their peculiarly intense atmosphere, their outbursts of eloquence, their sense of the world as an abyss made for falling into. That such testaments of deprivation and anxiety could have sustained a career as a paperback novelist is today cause for wonderment. Nothing so downbeat, so wedded to reiterations of personal and social failure, would be likely to find a mass market publisher at present. The absolutely personal voice of David Goodis seems almost to have escaped by accident. It emanated from the heart of an efficient entertainment industry, startlingly, like the wailing of an outcast.

Geoffrey O'Brien

Geoffrey O'Brien is the author of *Hardboiled America: The Lurid Years of Paperbacks*.

Chapter One

It was raining hard in Philadelphia as Cassidy worked the bus through heavy traffic on Market Street. He hated the street on these busy Saturday nights, especially during April when the rain came down hard and the traffic cops were annoyed with the rain and took it out on cabbies and bus drivers. Cassidy sympathized with the traffic cops and when they glared and yelled, he only shrugged and gestured helplessly. If they had a tough corner to patrol, he had a tough bus to steer. It was really a miserable bus, old and sick, and its transmission was constantly complaining.

The bus was one of three owned by a small company located on Arch Street. The three busses went north each day to Easton, then back again to Philadelphia. Back and forth between Easton and Philadelphia was a monotonous grind, but Cassidy needed the job badly, and a man with his background always found it difficult to obtain jobs.

Aside from the pay, it was emotionally important for Cassidy to do this type of work. Keeping his eyes on the road and his mind on the wheel was a protective fence holding him back from internal as well as external catastrophe.

The bus made a turn off Market Street, went up through the slashing rain to Arch, went into the depot. Cassidy climbed out, opened the door, stood there to help them down from the bus. He had the habit of studying their faces as they emerged, wondering what their thoughts were, and what their lives were made of. The old women and the girls, the frowning stout men with loose flesh hanging from their jaws, and the young men who gazed dully ahead as though seeing nothing. Cassidy looked at their faces and had an idea he could see the root of their trouble. It was the fact that they were ordinary people and they didn't know what real trouble was. He could tell them. He could damn well tell them.

1

The last of the passengers stepped off the bus and Cassidy moved across the narrow, damp waiting room, smoking a cigarette as he turned in his trip report to the supervisor. He walked out of the depot and took a streetcar down Arch, going east toward the river, the big dark sullen Delaware. He lived near the Delaware, in a three-room flat that overlooked Dock Street and the piers and the river.

The streetcar let Cassidy out and he ran to the corner newsstand and bought a paper. He held the slanted paper over his head as he hurried through the rain toward home. The neon sign of a small taproom caught his eye and for a moment he considered the idea of a shot. But he let it ride because what he needed right now was food. It was half-past nine and he hadn't had any food since noon. He should have eaten in Easton but some company genius had made an abrupt schedule change and there was no other driver available at the moment. Things like that were always happening to him. It was one of the many enjoyable aspects of driving a bus for a two-by-four outfit.

The rain was coming down very hard and he ran for it, He let the paper fly away through the rain and scooted the last few yards and leaped into the doorway of the tenement building. He was breathing hard and he was more than a little wet. But now it felt nice to be inside and climbing the stairway to his home.

He walked down the hall and opened the door of the flat and walked in. Then he stood motionless, gazing about. After that he blinked a few times. Then he went on staring.

The place was a complete wreck. The room looked as if it had been given a vigorous spin and turned upside down several times. Most of the furniture was overturned and the sofa had been sent crashing into a wall with enough force to bring down a lot of plaster and create a gaping hole. A small table was upside down. Two chairs had their legs broken off. Whisky bottles, some of them broken, most of them empty, were scattered all over the room. He took a long look at that. Then his eyes leaped. There was blood on the floor.

The blood was in little pools, a few threads of red here and there. The blood had dried but it was still shiny and the glimmer of it sent a burning spear through Cassidy's brain.

2

He told himself it was Mildred's blood. Something had happened to Mildred!

Countless times he had warned her against throwing these drinking parties while he was away on the bus route. They had fought about it. They had fought blazingly and sometimes physically, but he always had a feeling he couldn't win. In the core of his mind was the knowledge that he was getting exactly what he had bargained for. Mildred was a wild animal, a living chunk of dynamite that exploded periodically and caused Cassidy to explode, and these rooms were more of a battleground than a home. Yet, as he looked at the blood on the floor, he had a grinding, ripping fear that he had lost Mildred. The thought of it amounted to a kind of paralysis. All he could do was stand there and see the blood.

There was a noise behind him. The door had opened. He turned slowly, knowing somehow it was Mildred even before he saw her. She was closing the door and smiling at him, her eyes going into him, then past him, her moving hand indicating the wreckage of the room. The gesture was only partially drunken. He knew she had a lot of liquor in her, but she was rather gifted when it came to carrying her liquor, and she was always fully aware of what she was doing. Now she was challenging him. It was her way of stating she had decided to throw a party and the guests had wrecked the place and did he want to make something of it?

Silently he answered Mildred's silent question. He nodded very slowly. He took a step toward her and she didn't move. He took another step toward her, waiting for her to move. He raised his right arm and she stood there smiling at him. His arm sliced air and his flat palm arrived hard and cracking across her mouth.

Mildred lost the smile for only an instant. Then it was there again, the lips and eyes aimed not at Cassidy but toward the other side of the room. She walked slowly in that direction. She picked up an empty whisky bottle and pitched it at Cassidy's head.

It grazed the side of his head and he heard it crashing against the wall. He lunged at Mildred, but she had lifted another bottle and she was swinging it in little circles.

3

Cassidy threw up his arms protectively as he swerved away. He tripped over a fallen chair and went to the floor. Mildred moved toward him and he expected to feel the bottle coming down on his head. It was an excellent opportunity for Mildred and she never failed to take advantage of an opportunity.

But now, for some special reason that summed up as a puzzle, she chose to turn away from Cassidy, to walk slowly into the bedroom. As she closed the door Cassidy picked himself up, rubbed the side of his head where the other bottle had raised a lump, and felt in his pockets for a cigarette.

He couldn't find a cigarette. He moved aimlessly around the room, discovered a bottle that had a couple of drinks left in it, raised it to his lips and took the two drinks. Then he gazed at the bedroom door.

A feeling of vague uneasiness took root inside him and grew and sharpened and became acute. He knew he was disappointed because the battle hadn't continued. Of course, he told himself, that didn't make sense. But then there were very few elements in his life with Mildred that made sense. And lately, he recalled, there was absolutely nothing that made sense. It was getting worse all the time.

Cassidy shrugged. It wasn't much of a shrug. It was more of a sigh. He walked into the small kitchen and saw more wreckage. The sink was ready to collapse under the weight of empty bottles and filthy dishes. The table was a mess and the floor was worse. He opened the icebox and saw the sad remains of what he had expected would be his meal tonight. Slamming the door of the icebox, he could sense the uneasiness and disappointment going away and the rage coming back. A few loose cigarettes were on the table. He lit one, took several rapid puffs as he let his rage climb to high gear. When it reached that point, he barged into the bedroom.

Mildred stood at the dresser, leaning toward the mirror as she worked lipstick onto her mouth. She had her back turned to Cassidy and as she saw him in the mirror she leaned lower over the dresser, arching her back and emphasizing her big behind.

4

Cassidy said, "Turn around."

She arched her back a little more. "If I do, you won't see it."

"I ain't looking at it."

"You're always looking at it."

"I can't help that," Cassidy said. "It's so damn big I can't see anything else."

"Sure it's big." Her voice was syrupy and languid as she went on fixing her lips. "If it wasn't, it wouldn't interest you."

"Here's some news for you," Cassidy said. "I ain't interested."

"You're a liar." She turned very slowly and her body made a large smooth fat curving flow so that the sight of her as she faced him was thick and juicy, richly sweet and deliciously bitter. And as they stood there looking at each other the room was very quiet for Cassidy, his brain was quiet, containing only the knowledge of Mildred's presence, the colors of her, the lines of her. His eyes gulped and he was tasting the flavor of Mildred, his throat blocked as something heavy swirled in there and tried to prevent him from breathing. Damn her, he was saying to himself, goddamn her, and he tried to drag his eyes away from her and his eyes remained on her.

He was seeing the night-black hair of Mildred, the disordered shiny mass of heavy hair. He was seeing the brandy-colored eyes, long-lashed, very long-lashed. And the arrogant upward curve of her gorgeous nose. He was trying with all his power to hate the sight of her full fruitlike lips, and the maddening display of her immense breasts, the way they swept out, aimed at him like weapons. He stood looking at this woman to whom he had been married for almost four years, with whom he slept in the same bed every night, but what he saw was not a mate. He saw a harsh and biting and downright unbearable obsession.

Seeing it, knowing it for what it was, he was able to realize it was just that and nothing more. He told himself there was no use trying to make it anything more than what it was. He craved Mildred's body and he couldn't do without

5

it, and that was the one and only reason he went on living with her.

He was certain of that, and to the same degree he knew that Mildred had an identical feeling toward him. He had always been attractive to a certain type of woman, the hedonistic type, and it was because his body was powerful, thick, compact and very hard. At thirty-six he had the hardness packed into a stocky frame, the shoulders wide and muscular, the stomach flat and hard, the legs very thick and like rock. He knew that Mildred went for his looks, the wild curly wealth of pale blond hair, the dark gray eyes, the nose that had been broken twice but was still a good solid rugged nose. His skin was red and leathery and tough, and that was another thing Mildred liked. He nodded to himself, telling himself that aside from all these things, she hated his guts.

He was four years older than Mildred, yet, every now and then, he had the feeling of being much younger than she was, of being a blind and blundering young fool who'd been magnetized by a powerful and experienced female. Sometimes it worked the other way. He visualized himself as an old and battered wreck, lured by the luxurious haven of the luscious lips and breasts, revitalized by the springtime rhythm of her swinging hips.

She was swinging them now as she turned away and moved back to the dresser. She picked up the lipstick and resumed painting her mouth. Cassidy sat down on the edge of the bed, He took a final puff at the cigarette, let it fall to the floor and stepped on it. Then he took off his shoes, stretched out on the bed with his hands locked under his head, and waited for Mildred to come to the bed.

He waited a few minutes, not conscious of waiting because he was anticipating their being in bed together. He had his eyes closed and he could hear the rain banging away at the outside wall. There was something very special about making love when it was raining. The sound of the rain always had a certain wild effect on Mildred. Sometimes when it rained very hard she tore the hell out of him. In the summer, during electric storms, it seemed she snatched at the sky and used some of the lightning. He

6

started to think about that. He told himself to quit getting his kicks thinking about it, and abruptly he was impatient for Mildred to come to him.

Cassidy opened his eyes and saw her at the dresser. She was fixing her hair. He sat up and saw her nodding in approval at her face in the mirror. Then she was moving toward the door.

Cassidy swung his legs over the side of the bed. He tried to keep the shock and alarm from his voice as he said, "Where do you think you're going?"

"Out for the evening."

He moved rapidly, with a kind of frenzy. He took hold of her wrists. "You're staying here."

Mildred smiled at him. The smile was wide, showing her teeth. "You look like you need it bad."

His grip was hot metal around her wrists. He told himself to relax. She was only teasing him. Maybe it was some new technique to make him angry. She always seemed to enjoy him most when he was angry. He decided he wouldn't give her the satisfaction of seeing him hit the boiling point. His hands dropped away from her wrists and he shaped a nasty smile and said, "You got my looks wrong. All I need is food. I ain't had a meal since noon. Go in the kitchen and fix me supper."

"You're no cripple. Fix it yourself." Again she turned toward the door.

Cassidy grabbed her shoulders and swung her around. He couldn't hide his anger and it sizzled in his eyes, mixing with dismay as he said, "I pay rent here and I buy the food. When I come home at night, I'm entitled to a cooked meal."

Mildred didn't answer. She reached up and jerked his hands away from her shoulders. Them she pivoted fast and walked out of the bedroom. Cassidy followed her into the wrecked parlor, rushed past her and blocked the door.

"Nothing doing," he snarled. "I said you're staying here."

He was preparing himself for another battle. He wanted the battle to start here and now, to work its way across the room and then into the bedroom, to end there on the bed

7

with the sound of the rain outside. Like their battles always ended, whether it rained or not. But tonight it was raining hard and it would be one of their special battles.

Mildred didn't move. She didn't say anything. She just looked at him. He was sure now that some new and disturbing development had taken place and again he had the hollow feeling of uneasiness.

His eyes dropped to the floor, He saw the blood, and he waved his hand toward it and said, "Who belongs to that?"

She shrugged. "Somebody's nose, Or mouth. I don't know. My friends got into an argument."

"I told you to keep your friends out of here."

Mildred rested her weight on one leg. She put her hands on her hips. "Tonight," she said, "we're not going to fight about it."

Her tone was strangely detached, and Cassidy said slowly, "What is it? What's the matter?"

She backed away. It wasn't retreat. It was just to get a good look at him. She said, "You, Cassidy. You're what's the matter, I'm fed up with you."

He blinked a few times. He tried to think of something to say but he couldn't get any ideas. Finally he murmured, "Go on. Say it."

"You got ears? I'm saying it, I'm just fed up with you, that's all."

"For what good reason?"

She smiled at him. It was almost a pitying smile. "You figure it out."

"Now listen," he said, "I don't like these puzzle games. That's one thing you've never tried before and I won't let you start now. If you've got a beef, I want to know what it is."

She didn't reply. Not even a look. Her eyes rested on the wall behind him, as though she were alone in the room. He wanted to say something to re-establish verbal contact but something blocked his brain. He didn't know what it was and he had no desire to know what it was. The only desire was a throbbing urge that blasted at him from the rainstorm outside and the lush and luscious female shape that was here in the room with him.

He took a step toward her. She looked at him and knew what his plans were. She shook her head and said, "Not tonight. I'm not in the mood."

It sounded strange. She had never used that phrase before. He wondered if she really meant it. The room was cold with quiet as he stared at her and realized that she did mean it.

He took another step toward her. She didn't budge and he told himself she was waiting for him to lay hands on her and then she would start to fight. That would be it. That would start the flame going. They'd have one hell of a hot battle and it would be blazing action in the bed. Then it would be as if she couldn't get enough of him and he wouldn't be able to pull away. And that was all right. That was fine.

The sound of the rainstorm clanged in his head and he reached out and took hold of her wrist. He pulled her toward him and in that instant he felt the full impact of amazement and dismay. There was no fight. There was no resistance. Her face was expressionless, and she looked at him as though he had no identity.

Very deep inside of him a warning voice told him to let go of her, to leave her alone. When a woman wasn't in the mood she just wasn't in the mood. And when it was that way, there was nothing worse than forcing the issue.

But now that his hand was gripping her flesh he couldn't let go. He forgot that she wasn't putting up a fight, that her body was limp and passive as he took her into the bedroom. He was aware only of the bulging breasts, the rounded luxury of the hips and thighs, the presence that sent high voltage through every nerve and fiber of his being. He wanted this and he was going to have it and there was no other matter involved.

He pushed her toward the bed and she fell onto it like something inanimate. Her face remained expressionless as she looked up at him. It was as though she were miles and miles away from what he was doing. He began to sense a sickeningly futile frenzy in his efforts to excite her. She just rested there flat on her back like a big rag doll and let him do as he pleased. He tried to be enraged and once he raised his hand to hit her, to get some kind of response, any kind, but he knew it wouldn't do any good. She wouldn't even feel it.

And yet, although the knowledge of her indifference was almost a physical agony, the roaring fire inside him had far greater power, and the only thing he could do was surrender himself to it. As he took his woman, the fire was solely his own fire and there was the sordid and dismal feeling, and finally the downright horrible feeling, of being alone in the bed.

Then, some moments later, he was actually alone in the bed and he heard Mildred moving around in the parlor. He climbed out of bed, quickly put his clothes on and walked into the parlor. Mildred was lighting a cigarette. She puffed at it slowly, took it out of her mouth and gazed thoughtfully at the burning tobacco. Cassidy waited for her to say something.

She had nothing to say. He discovered that it was impossible for him to interpret her attitude. The quiet was bothering him and gradually it became worse and eventually he had the notion that the floor was giving way. He groped in his brain, trying to remember if anything like this had ever before happened between them. Everything else had happened, but never quite like this.

Presently she looked at him. In a matter-of-fact way, she said, "Today's my birthday. That's why I threw the party."

"Oh." Cassidy's face was blank for a long moment. Then he tried a smile. "I knew you were sore about something. I guess I should have remembered."

He reached into his pants pocket and came up with a ten-dollar bill. He widened the smile as he handed her the money and said, "Buy yourself something."

She gazed down at the ten-dollar bill in her palm and said, "What's this?"

"It's a birthday present."

"You sure about that?" Her voice was low and calm. "Maybe you're just paying me a fee for what happened in the bedroom. If that's the case, I wouldn't want you to cheat yourself. It wasn't worth a thin dime."

She crumpled the bill and threw it in Cassidy's face. Then

she had the door open and, while Cassidy stood there blinking, she ran out.

Chapter Two

In the kitchen, Cassidy tried to clean up the mess of bottles and dishes and stale food. After a while he gave it up, decided he was starving and maybe there was enough in the icebox to help an empty stomach. He warmed some potatoes and buttered a roll, but when he had the food ready on the table, he couldn't look at it.

Maybe coffee would help. He lit a fire under the percolator and sat down at the table and stared at the floor. He turned his head slowly and gazed out the kitchen window. The rain was letting up and he could hear its weak patter on walls and rooftops. If it rained for an entire month it wouldn't begin to clean these miserable tenements, he thought. The ugly cobbled streets like a pock-marked face. And the people. The water-front bums. The human ruins. A perfect specimen was right here in this kitchen.

The coffee was bubbling. He filled a cup and let the hot black sugarless liquid seep down his throat. It tasted awful. Well, it wasn't the coffee's fault. The mood he was in, anything would taste awful. Even champagne would taste like soapy water. Now what had made him think of champagne? Something had taken him back along the channels of the past, to a time when he had a taste for champagne, when he had the money to afford it. He tried to put the thought out of his mind.

But memory was growing there, working on him. He saw the steam coming up from the coffee and in the steam the entire business was taking place again, as though projected from an invisible lantern. Cassidy was going back, and back, very far back to the little town in Oregon, and the little house with the little lawn, and the little bicycle. He was back there in the wonderful, glowing days of high school and the roaring grandstands and James Cassidy going in at right guard to plug the hole in the line. And later, James Cassidy at the University of Oregon. At graduation, the yearbook had very nice things to say—"Brilliant achievement in the halls of learning and on the gridiron. Majoring in mechanical engineering, James Cassidy is third highest man in the class. In his final season on the Webfoot eleven, he was selected All-Pacific-Coast Conference guard."

Solid, clean-cut James Cassidy. A credit to the old home town. And they said it again in 1943, when he came home after his fiftieth mission. And then he went back to England and piloted the B-24 through another thirty missions. When the big show was over he had his mind made up about his future, and the airline company in New York was only too willing to put him on the payroll.

A four-engine job. Eighty passengers. The vast green expanse of La Guardia Airport. The smooth, precise schedule of operations. Flight 634 coming in, on time. Captain J. Cassidy reporting. Here's your pay check. A year of it, two years, three years, and then they put him on the transatlantic run. Fifteen thousand a year. In New York he had an apartment in the East Seventies, he wore $125 suits when he wasn't in the sky, he was invited to the better parties, and several of the more elegant post-debutantes were wishing he would look in their direction.

When it happened, the authorities said it was inexcusable. The newspapers called it one of the worst tragedies in the history of aviation. The big plane was taking off, getting into the air at the far end of the field, when it had suddenly nosed over to crash in the marshes and instantly explode. Of the seventy-eight passengers and the crew, there were only eleven survivors. And the only surviving crew member was the pilot, Captain J. Cassidy.

At the hearing, they just stared at him and he knew they didn't believe him. Nothing he could say would make them believe him. But it was true. It was dreadfully true that the copilot had suffered a sudden emotional collapse, the kind that gives no warning, the ghastly fusing of negative elements that causes a man to break up as earth breaks up when a quake hits. The copilot had turned on Cassidy, pulled him away from the controls, grabbed the controls, and sent the plane downward when it was less than a hundred feet in the air.

The authorities sat there and listened, and then without saying a word they were calling Cassidy a liar. The newspapers said he was worse than a liar. They said he was trying to fix the blame on an innocent dead man. The family of the dead man insisted there was not the slightest trace of emotional instability, and certainly no reason for a sudden breakdown, and they demanded that Cassidy be punished. A great many people were demanding that Cassidy be punished, especially when someone offered the information that Cassidy had attended a champagne party the night before the accident.

That was the way they explained it. They brought in experts to elaborate on the physiological effect of champagne. Stressing the fact that champagne is tricky in its aftereffects; that a man can drink a glass of water on the morning after and start getting drunk again. They put it that way. They said that was it. They told Cassidy he was finished.

He couldn't believe it. He tried to fight it. But they wouldn't listen. They wouldn't even look at him. It was bad enough in New York, but when it happened in the little town in Oregon he began to realize the full impact of personal tragedy. A week after he left Oregon he started to drink.

There were times when he fought with all his power to stop the drinking, and on some of these occasions he succeeded, and he went out and looked for work. But his name and his face had appeared in papers across the nation, and they told him to get out and get out fast. Once they tried to throw him out bodily and it ended in a brawl and he spent a week in jail.

The downhill process was steep and rapid. During a chaotic stretch of drinking, he decided the hell with all of them, and went to Nevada and started to gamble. He had saved a little more than ten thousand dollars from his years with the airline, and in Nevada, at the dice tables, it took him exactly four days to lose every cent. When he left Nevada, his means of transportation was a freight train.

Nevada to Texas, and he found work on the Galveston

water front. But someone recognized him and there was another fight, and he came out of it with a broken nose. In New Orleans he did ten days for vagrancy, and in Mobile he put three men and himself in the hospital and then did sixty days for assault and battery. In Atlanta it was vagrancy again and he was put with the chain gang for twelve days. He talked back to a guard and got his nose broken for the second time and had three teeth knocked out. In North Carolina he hopped a freight that took him to Philadelphia and he spent a few weeks in the tenderloin around Eighth and Race, then tried the water front for a job. He found part-time work as a stevedore, rented a small room near the docks, and begged himself to stay put and keep working and quit drinking.

But he hated the work and he hated the room, and because he had reached the point where he was hating himself, he decided he needed the drinking. During his third week on the job he walked into a water-front saloon named Lundy's Place, an establishment of dirty floor and cracked walls and disorganized human beings. He ordered a shot of rye. He ordered another shot. He was on his third drink when he saw the bright purple dress and the way it bulged and the way she was sitting there, looking at him.

He walked toward the table. She was sitting there alone. He asked her what she was looking at. Mildred said he'd be a lot prettier if he had a few more teeth in his mouth. He told her how he had lost the teeth. Eight or nine drinks later he was telling her everything. When he was finished with it, he looked at her and waited for her reaction.

Her reaction was a shrug. A few nights later, when he asked her to come to his room, she shrugged again and got up and they walked out together.

On the following day, Cassidy visited a dentist and was measured for a bridge of three teeth. Within a month the teeth were fitted nicely in his mouth and he was married to Mildred. Their honeymoon was a five-cent ferry ride across the Delaware River to Camden. A few days later, Mildred told him to go out and look for a full-time job. She said he might be able to find work with one of the small bus companies on Arch Street. Cassidy took a walk up Arch Street

14

and went into the depot and knew it was the kind of outfit that has trouble staying on its feet. He knew they weren't going to ask him a lot of questions about himself. The questions they did ask were easily answered. He gave them his right name, his right address, and when they asked him about his previous bus-driving experience, there was no need to lie. At college, he'd worked part-time as driver of a school bus.

They said all right, and that afternoon they gave him a cap and he took eighteen passengers to Easton. He came back that night to tell Mildred of his good luck, but instead of going directly to the flat, he decided to stop in at Lundy's Place for a drink. Approaching Lundy's he saw Mildred and a few other women and men come staggering out, all drunk as blazes. In that moment he laughed deep inside himself, knowing it was a case of what the hell, it didn't matter, he couldn't expect anything better. The important thing was, he had the bus. It wasn't as big as a four-engined plane, but it was a rolling machine, and it had wheels. And he was at the controls. That was the thing that mattered. That was what he needed. More than anything. He knew he had lost the ability to control Cassidy, and certainly he would never be able to control Mildred, but there was one thing left in this world that he could and would control. The one thing that was real, that had meaning and stability and purpose. The thing that allowed him to grip a wheel and shift gears and come as close as he would ever come to the dimly remembered days of piloting a liner in the sky. It was only an old, battered, broken-down bus, but it was a damn good bus. It was a wonderful bus. Because it would do what he wanted it to do. Because once again J. Cassidy was in the driver's seat.

He had felt good about it that night and now, as he looked down at the steaming black coffee, he managed to capture some of that same feeling. He still had the bus. He was still in the driver's seat. He was still in charge of the passengers. At Lundy's he was just another bum, and in these rooms he was merely another creature of the water front, but in the bus, goddamnit, he was the driver, he was the captain. They were depending on him to get them to

Easton. And in Easton they depended on him to bring the bus safely to Philadelphia. They needed him behind the wheel.

He'd have a drink on that. He hurried into the parlor and found a bottle with some whisky in it and took a generous gulp. He expanded his chest and took another drink. A toast to the captain of the ship, the pilot of the plane, the driver of the bus. Now then, a toast to Captain J. Cassidy. And a toast to the four wheels of the bus. Or better yet, drink a toast to each wheel. Everybody drink. Come on, everybody. Drink! Drink!

Cassidy threw the empty bottle at the wall. It crashed and he saw the spray of flying glass. He laughed wildly and lurched out of the flat. It had stopped raining but the streets were still wet, and he grinned at the glimmering pavement as he staggered along the water front toward Lundy's Place.

Chapter Three

He moved toward Lundy's with his mind dampened and softened, the whisky fumes swirling in his head and dulling his eyes. There was no thought or purpose other than the fact that he was on his way to Lundy's to have a drink. To have several drinks. As many drinks as he wanted. And nothing would prevent him from getting where he was going. He was on his way to have himself some liquor and they'd better not get in his way. He had no idea who "they" represented, but whoever "they" were, "they" would do well to tend to their own business and give Cassidy a clear path ahead to Lundy's Place.

On the river side of Dock Street the big ships rocked gently on the black water like monstrous hens, fat and complacent in their roosts. Their lights twinkled and threw blobs of yellow on the cobbled street bordering the piers. Across Dock Street the stalls of the fish market were shuttered and dark, except for cracks of light from within, where purveyors of Delaware shad and Barnegat crab and clam and

Ocean City flounder were preparing their merchandise for the early-morning trade. As Cassidy passed the fish market, a shutter opened and a mess of fish guts came sailing out, aimed at a large rubbish can. The fish guts missed the can and landed against Cassidy's leg.

Cassidy moved toward the opened shutter and glowered at the fat, sweaty face above a white apron.

"You," Cassidy said. "You look where you're throwin' things."

"Aw, shut up," the fish merchant said. He started to close the shutter.

Cassidy grabbed the shutter and held it open. "Who you tellin' to shut up?"

Another face appeared within the stall. Cassidy saw the two faces as a double-headed monstrosity. The two faces looked at each other amd the fat face said, "It ain't nothin'. Just that liquored-up bum, that Cassidy."

A hand reached out to close the shutter. Cassidy kept it open. "All right," he said, "so I'm liquored up. So what? You want to make an argument out of it?"

"Go on, Cassidy. Go on, take a walk. Go on down to Lundy's with the rest of the slime."

"Slime?" Cassidy jerked hard on the shutter so that its hinges whined in protest. "Come out here and call me slime. Come on out here!"

"Whatsa matter, Cassidy? You aggravated? You have another fight with your wife?"

"Leave my wife out of this." He pulled harder on the shutter. The hinges began to give way.

The fat face became alarmed and angry. "Let go that shutter, you drunk bastard—"

"Oh," Cassidy said, and he laughed. "Is that what I am? I didn't know. Thanks for telling me." He gave a vicious yank at the shutter and the hinges came away from the wall. He staggered back with the weight of it. The two faces were emerging from the stall window. Cassidy hurled the shutter at them and they withdrew with a split second to spare as the shutter went flying into the stall. Cassidy heard the crash, the shouts and curses. He knew they wouldn't come out after him because a similar incident had

17

happened once before, and on that occasion he had closed the left eye of the fat man and knocked the other man unconscious. In a way he regretted that they weren't coming out. He as itching for a solid session of violence.

He turned away from the fish stall and continued down the pavement. The issue with the shutter had sobered him sufficiently so that he had a better perspective of what his plans were. His plans focused more on Mildred than on additional liquor. He intended to find her in Lundy's Place, drag her out of there, take her home, and force her to cook him a decent meal. Goddamnit, a man who did a hard day's work had a right to a decent meal. And then in the bed. The identity of Mildred was erased as he thought of the bed and what would happen in the bed. In terms of what would happen, of what he would be doing and with whom he would be doing it, there was no thought of Mildred, only the thought of Mildred's physical equipment.

And yet, thinking in those terms, he was hit again with the uneasiness, the puzzlement. His brain continued to clear as he recalled her unusual behavior, the fact that she had refused battle, had walked out in the middle of an argument. She had never done that before. What was wrong with her? What new trick was she trying to pull?

He stopped his forward progress and leaned heavily against a brick wall. Better think about this. Better try to get it clear. It wasn't anything to pass over lightly. It was a serious matter. Came under the heading of what they called a domestic problem. Sure, after all, this woman Mildred was married to him. She was his wife. The ring on her finger could be hocked for two bucks, but it was a wedding ring and it had been put there in the presence of a bona fide justice of the peace. A legal ceremony at three in the morning in Elkton, Maryland. According to law and according to God's will, as the man had said. Nothing underhanded about it. A completely legitimate marriage and she was his lawfully wedded wife and he had his rights and she'd better wise up to that and not get any fancy ideas.

Anyway, what was she beefing about? He brought home his money each week, paid the rent on time, saw to it that

18

she had clothes to put on her back. If part of the cash went for liquor, it was by mutual consent, and she drank as much as he did, sometimes more. Come to think of it, when it came to finances she was gaining much the better part of the bargain, because she was always getting part-time jobs as a hairdresser and he never questioned her about the money she made. Chances were, she spent every dime on whisky, as she'd probably been doing before he met her.

What in God's name was she beefing about? She'd given him as many black eyes as he'd given her. Perhaps more, although the black eyes had been too numerous to record. He wished he had a shiny nickel for every time she'd aimed correctly with a plate or a dish pan or an empty whisky bottle. On one notable occasion the whisky bottle hadn't been empty and he had to have three stitches put in his scalp.

His thoughts waded through the shallows. There were deeper channels waiting for his thoughts but he was never inclined to probe that far down when it came to Mildred. He made it a point to think of the woman and himself in terms of fundamentals and nothing else. Because everything else was too complicated and he'd been dragged through enough trouble without bringing in further complications.

And yet, as he came nearer to Lundy's Place, as he saw the dirty yellow glow flowing from the unscrubbed window of the saloon, he felt a stab of acute self-doubt. He was assailed by a sharp fear concerning Mildred. And suddenly he knew what it was. Mildred had found another man!

With equal suddenness he knew the identity of the man and he understood why Mildred had been pulled in that particular direction. Telling himself he should have suspected long ago, he pressed buttons in his brain to bring back scenes and episodes he'd more or less ignored at the time of their occurrence. Although most men who saw Mildred for the first time were prone to widen their eyes and breathe hard, it had been especially noticeable in the case of a man named Haney Kenrick. The factor that made Kenrick a special candidate was the cash in his pockets. It wasn't a fortune, but it far exceeded the financial capabilities of all the other men who patronized Lundy's Place.

And so that was it. Cassidy nodded emphatically. It was just as clear and simple as that. It was so easy to figure it was almost funny. Easy to understand why she'd said she was fed up with him. Of course she was fed up. Fed up with cheap dresses and five-dollar shoes. And dimestore cosmetics. Fed up with the dingy rooms above the water front. Now he knew why she'd thrown the ten-dollar bill in his face. It wasn't enough. And his mind became a canvas on which he roughly, furiously painted Haney Kenrick's hand, a fifty-dollar bill extended, and Mildred taking the money.

Cassidy strode toward Lundy's Place with his arms bent outward at his sides, his fists clenched.

Lundy's Place had the appearance of something projected through old film onto a cracked screen. It was large and it had a high ceiling and the furnishings had no color, no gloss, no definite shape. The wood of the bar and tables was splintered and gray with time, amd the floor had a mossy texture, like woven dust. Lundy himself was only another furnishing, something old and dull and hollow, moving from bar to table, moving back and forth behind the bar with a face of stone. Most of the regular customers sat at the tables, at the same table and in the same chair night after night after night. And Cassidy, standing outside and peering through the fogged window, knew exactly where to look.

He saw Mildred seated at Haney Kenrick's table. Just the two of them sitting there, Kenrick talking energetically and Mildred smiling and nodding. Then Kenrick put his hand on Mildred's arm and leaned forward just a little and said something close to Mildred's ear. Mildred threw her head back and laughed.

Cassidy hunched his shoulders, lowered his head until it pressed hard against the window. He was able to remain still, knowing if he gave way now to what he wanted to do, he would crash through the window. He begged himself to relax. He told himself to wait out here and think it over.

But his eyes remained riveted to the table where she sat with Haney Kenrick. She was still laughing. And then Kenrick said something that made her laugh even harder.

They were laughing together. Cassidy quivered there at the window and studied the table as though it were an enemy trench eight or nine yards away.

On several occasions, and directly to the man's face, Cassidy had called Haney Kenrick a no-good slob. It had little to do with appearance, although Kenrick weighed more than two hundred pounds and it looked to be mostly blubber. The man was a couple of inches above medium height and always tried to make it more than that when he stood up. He always tried to get the weight up from his paunch and into his chest but after a few minutes it would go down again.

Cassidy narrowed his focus so that his eyes centered on Kenrick, and he saw Kenrick's fat, shiny face, the sparse light-brown hair greased down and across a rounded scalp. He saw Kenrick's attire, cheap and loud, the collar heavily starched, the suit pressed to blade sharpness, the shoes polished so they looked like enamel.

Haney Kenrick was forty-three and made his living selling household goods door-to-door on an installment basis. He lived in a room a few blocks away from Lundy's Place and it was his claim that he loved the water front and he loved Lundy's Place and all the dear, fine friends he had there.

The dear, fine friends all knew it was a lie. Kenrick was not accepted in most circles, and coming to Lundy's gave him a feeling of ego-satisfaction and superiority. He was never quite able to hide his disdain and contempt, and when he offered them a big hello and a pat on the back they just sat there and tolerated him and silently asked him who did he think he was fooling?

And there she was, sitting there with that fat faker. Playing up to him. Laughing at his jokes. Letting him get his blubbery face close to her. Letting his hand move up along her arm, toward the fleshy part where he could grab a cheap feel. Cassidy bit the side of his mouth and told himself it was time to barge in.

Something pulled the reins on him. He had no idea what it was, but he knew somehow it was connected with a kind of strategy. He dragged his eyes away from the table where

21

she sat with Kenrick, sent his attention toward the other tables, arrived finally at four drinkers who sat in a far corner at a table where there were usually three.

Three of his closest friends. There was Spann, a waterfront idler, lean and tricky but straight as a slide rule with people he liked. And Spann's girl friend, Pauline, with a shape like a toothpick and a face the color of a blank newspaper. There was Shealy, white-haired at forty, with an amazing capacity for liquor, with a brain that had once turned out college textbooks on economics. These days Shealy made his living from behind the counter of a ship chandlery off Dock Street. He was a good salesman for a place of that sort because he never tried to sell. He never tried to do anything. All he did was sit and drink. It was all any of them did, sitting there in the murky stagnation of Lundy's Place. A port for rudderless boats.

The fourth member of the party was someone Cassidy had never seen before. A small, fragile, pale woman. She looked to be somewhere in her late twenties. Cassidy saw her plainness, her mildness. Something kind and sweet. Something sanitary. And yet, as he watched her, as he saw the way she raised her glass, he knew instantly she was an alcoholic.

It showed. He could always tell. They gave themselves away in hundreds of little gestures. He never felt sorry for them because he was always too busy feeling sorry for himself. But now he felt a wave of pity for the pale-faced, yellow-haired woman who sat there with Shealy and Pauline and Spann. He decided it was important to find out who she was.

He entered Lundy's Place, walked slowly, almost casually across the room, and said hello to Shealy. He smiled dimly at Pauline and Spann and then he gazed at the fragile woman and waited for her to notice him. She was concentrating on a water glass half-filled with whisky. He knew she wasn't being rude. It was just that she couldn't take her eyes off the whisky.

"It stop raining?" Shealy said.

Cassidy nodded.

"Anything new?" Shealy asked.

Cassidy pulled a chair to the table, sat down and beckoned to Lundy. The old man came over and Cassidy ordered a fifth of rye. The fragile woman looked at Cassidy and smiled and Cassidy smiled back. He noticed her eyes were a pale gray. She was sort of pretty.

Shealy said, "Her name's Doris."

"What's his name?" Doris asked.

"His name is Cassidy," Shealy said.

"Does Mr. Cassidy drink?" Doris wanted to know.

"Sometimes," Cassidy said.

"I drink all the time," Doris said.

Shealy smiled at her as if he were her father. "Go on, child, go on with your drinking." He looked at Cassidy intently, then inclined his head toward the table where Mildred sat with Haney Kenrick. He said, "What is it, Jim? What's going on?"

Cassidy rested his hands on his lap. "She's having some drinks with Haney Kenrick. That's all I know."

Pauline said, "That ain't all I know."

Spann narrowed his eyes at Pauline and said, "You shut up. You hear? Sit there and shut up."

"You can't tell me to shut up!" Pauline said.

Spann's voice had the texture of kidskin. "I'm telling you. I get annoyed when you butt in where you're not concerned."

"I am concerned," Pauline said. "Cassidy here is my friend. I don't like to see my friends loused up."

Spann rubbed fingers across fingernails. "I think I'd better make her shut up."

"Leave her alone," Shealy said. "No matter what you do, she'll say it anyway sooner or later. Let her say it."

Lundy came to the table with the bottle. Cassidy paid for the liquor, opened the bottle and refilled the glasses. He put a jigger quantity into Doris' glass and smiled at her as she continued to hold the glass, waiting for more. He half-filled the glass and she waited with it and he had to fill the glass almost to the top before she nodded.

Pauline said, "You listen, Cassidy. You listen carefully. We were up at your place today. Mildred threw a party."

Cassidy leaned an elbow on the table and rubbed the

23

back of his head. "I found that out for myself."

"And the fight?" Pauline asked.

"I figured there was a fight," Cassidy said. And just as he said it, he noticed a slight swelling and redness at the base of Shealy's nose. His lips were pressed thin as he said, "Who hit you, Shealy?"

"I'll tell you who hit him," Pauline said. "That greasy pig sitting there with your wife."

Cassidy put both hands flat on the table.

"Now, easy, Jim," Shealy said. "Let it ride easy."

Pauline had her arms folded, her head bent toward Cassidy. "And I'll tell you why it happened. Kenrick had his hands all over Mildred. Squeezing and feeling like he was pricing oranges. And Mildred? She just stood there and let him do it—"

"That isn't quite true," Shealy interrupted. "Mildred was drunk and she didn't know what was happening."

"Like hell she didn't," Pauline said. "She was right there with it and if you want my opinion, she was enjoying it."

Spann smiled gently at Pauline and said, "Keep it up. Just keep it up. Before the night's over I'll tear your hair out by the roots."

"You won't do a thing," Pauline told him. "You're a zero. If you were one-tenth of a man you'd have proved it today when Kenrick began hitting Shealy. And all you did was look, like you had a ringside seat."

Shealy smiled at Cassidy. "I guess I dropped some blood on your floor."

"It was awful," Pauline said. "Shealy wasn't looking for no trouble. All he did was make a polite request. Like the fine gentleman he is. You are, Shealy, you're a real gentleman."

Shealy shrugged. "I merely asked Kenrick to stop what he was doing. I pointed out that Mildred was intoxicated—"

"And Kenrick only laughed," Pauline cut in. "Then Shealy told him again. Without any warning, he banged Shealy in the face."

Cassidy pulled his chair a few inches out from the table. He gazed across the room at Mildred and Haney Kenrick. He held the gaze until Kenrick saw him and smiled expan-

24

sively, waved a congenial hello, and waved again to let him know he was invited over to have a drink.

"Easy," Shealy said. "Easy, Jim."

"Only one thing bothers me," Cassidy murmured. "I don't like the fact that he hit you."

"It was nothing," Shealy said. He gave a little laugh. "Just a punch in the nose."

Pauline leaned toward Cassidy. "What about Mildred? You heard what he was doing with Mildred."

Cassidy looked down at his hands. "The hell with Mildred."

"She's your wife," Pauline said.

Doris smiled at Cassidy and said, "May I have another drink?"

He poured another drink for Doris. Some of it spilled on the table and he heard Pauline saying, "You hear me, Cassidy? I'm telling you something. She's your wife."

"That ain't the issue," Cassidy said. "It don't matter." He lifted his glass and took a heavy swig. He took another swig and emptied the glass and filled it again and then for a while it was quiet while all of them concentrated on their drinking. The interlude of quiet was like a strange lack of noise on the deck of a slowly sinking ship, with strangely unexcited people climbing into lifeboats. They were unaware of one another, quietly concentrating on their drinking.

Finally Pauline said, "That's what I claim. Shealy is a real gentleman."

"I wonder," Shealy said.

"You are." Pauline had tears in her eyes. "You are, you dear man."

Spann smiled at empty air. "And what about me?" he inquired. "What am I?"

"You're a lizard," Pauline said. She looked at Doris. "For Christ's sake, say something."

Doris lifted her glass and took a long, slow drink as though it were cool water.

Cassidy stood up. He stood steady, feeling the balance of his stance, hearing Shealy saying, "Easy, Jim. Please, now. Easy."

"I'm fine," Cassidy said.

25

"Don't," Shealy said. "I beg you, Jim. Please sit down."

"It's all right."

"No, Jim."

"He hit you. Ain't that what he did?"

"Please." Shealy tugged at Cassidy's sleeve.

"But don't you see?" Cassidy spoke softly. "You're my friend, Shealy. Times you talk like a book and you get on my nerves, but you're my friend. You're a no-good drunken wreck, but you're my friend and he had no right to hit you."

He took Shealy's hand away from his sleeve. He walked across the room, walking straight toward the table where they sat. Kenrick saw him coming, smiled widely, very widely. Mildred turned to see what Kenrick was smiling at, and she saw Cassidy and looked at him only for a moment, then turned her back to him.

Cassidy arrived at the table and Kenrick half-stood, reached for a chair and said, "What took you so long? We been waiting for you. Here, sit down. Have a drink."

"All right," Cassidy said. And Kenrick called to Lundy for a bottle and another glass.

Then Kenrick slapped Cassidy's shoulder and said, "Well, Jim old boy, how's it going?"

"Fine," Cassidy said.

"How's the old bus running?"

"O. K." He was looking at Mildred and she was looking back at him.

"How's things up in Easton?" Kenrick said, and again he slapped Cassidy's shoulder.

"It's a nice town," Cassidy said.

"That's what I hear." Kenrick's thick fingers played with a cigarette lighter. "I hear Easton's a great old town. They tell me it's good for installment routes."

"I wouldn't know," Cassidy said.

"Well," and Kenrick leaned back in his chair, "I'll tell you. I figure in terms of the number of streets. Low income bracket. Factory people. A lot of kids. That's what does it. You put your facts together, you size up an area, and you go out and sell."

"I don't know a thing about it," Cassidy said.

"It's something to learn," Kenrick stated. "It's very interesting."

"Not for me," Cassidy said. "I just drive a bus."

"And good hard honest work it is, too." Once more Kenrick slapped Cassidy's shoulder. "Not a thing to be ashamed of. It's just good plain simple hard honest work."

Lundy came to the table with the bottle and the glass and Kenrick poured three drinks. He lifted his glass and opened his mouth to say something, quickly changed his mind and went on lifting the glass. But Cassidy's hand touched his arm to delay the drinking.

"Say it, Haney."

"Say what?"

"The toast." Cassidy was smiling, at Mildred. "The toast you were going to say."

"What toast?"

"To Mildred. To Mildred's birthday."

Kenrick's mouth worked as though he were trying to hide chewing gum under his lip. "Birthday?" It came out nervously fast.

"Sure," Cassidy said. "Didn't you know it was her birthday?"

"Well, yes. Yes, of course." Kenrick's laugh had gurgling in it. He raised his glass ceremoniously and said, "To Mildred's birthday."

"And Mildred's arms," Cassidy said.

Kenrick stared at him.

"Mildred's soft white arms," Cassidy said. "Nice soft juicy arms."

Kenrick tried to laugh again but no sound came out.

"And Mildred's development up front. Take a look at that development. Look at them, Haney."

"Well, now really, Jim—"

"Look at them. Take a look at them. Tremendous, ain't they?"

Kenrick swallowed hard.

"Look at the way her hips curve out," Cassidy said. "Look at that pair of hips. Big and full and round. Look at all that gorgeous meat. Ever see anything like it?"

There was sweat on Kenrick's face.

27

"Go on, Haney, Look. Keep looking. She's right there. You can see her. You can touch her. Reach out and touch her. Put your hands on her. I ain't stopping you. Put your hands all over her. Go on, Haney."

Kenrick swallowed again. He managed to assume a solemn, stern expression and he said, "Now stop it, Jim. This woman is your wife."

"When did you find out?" Cassidy asked. "Did you know it this afternoon?"

Mildred stood up. "That's enough, Cassidy."

"You sit down," he told her. "Keep quiet."

"Cassidy," she said, "you're blind drunk and you better get out of here before you start a riot."

"He'll be all right," Kenrick said.

"He's blind, stinking drunk," Mildred said. "He's a mess."

"Sure I am." It crashed as it came from Cassidy's lips. "A good-for-nothing drunken bum. Not good enough for you. Don't make enough money. Can't buy you things you want. You know I'll never be anything more than what I am. You figure you can get something better. Like this here," and he indicated Haney Kenrick.

Kenrick's eyes probed Cassidy's drunkenness. It occurred to Kenrick that Cassidy was really quite drunk and might not be too much trouble. Kenrick also sensed that a ripe opportunity was presenting itself. He saw a means of increasing his stature in Mildred's eyes.

Kenrick said, "Go home, Jim. Go home and sleep."

Cassidy laughed. "If I go home, where will you go with her?"

"Don't worry about that," Kenrick said.

"You can be goddamn sure I won't worry." Cassidy stood up. "I won't give it a thought. Why should I? What do I care what she does? You think I'm sore because you put your hands on her today? I ain't sore about that at all. To me it don't matter. I tell you it don't matter."

"All right," Mildred said. "You're telling us it don't matter. Now what else?"

"Let's leave it alone," Kenrick said. "He'll be all right. He'll behave himself and he'll go home." Kenrick stood up and took Cassidy's arm in a strong grip and started to lead him away from the table. Cassidy pulled away, lost his balance, bumped into another table and fell to the floor. Kenrick reached down, pulled him upright, and continued leading him toward the door. Once again he jerked away from Kenrick's grasp.

"Now, be nice, Jim."

Cassidy blinked, gazed past Kenrick and saw Mildred moving toward the table where Shealy and the others sat. He saw Mildred reaching out to grab Pauline's wrist.

He heard Mildred saying, "All right, troublemaker. You're not happy unless you have your mouth open. Now I'll close it for you."

Mildred yanked Pauline to her feet and smacked her hard across the face. Pauline cursed and snatched at Mildred's hair, and Mildred launched another smack that sent Pauline against the wall, to bounce away and run into another smack across the mouth. Pauline screeched like a wild bird and flew at Mildred and Shealy was trying to move in between them. Kenrick had turned and was watching it, and as Shealy attempted to separate the women, Kenrick commanded, "Stay out of it, Shealy."

Shealy ignored the command. Kenrick took a few steps toward Shealy and at that point Cassidy said, "Turn around, Haney. Look at me. You had your fun with Shealy this afternoon. Tonight you'll have it with me."

There was a cold precision and finality in Cassidy's tone, and it caused everyone in the room to stare at Cassidy. The combat between Mildred and Pauline had ended with Pauline sobbing on the floor. Spann was ignoring Pauline and watching Cassidy and waiting to see what Cassidy meant to do. They were all wondering what Cassidy was going to do.

Kenrick looked worried. It seemed that Cassidy had somehow sobered himself. Kenrick didn't like the way Cassidy stood there, legs straight and firmly planted, arms swimming just a little, with the hands clenched so that the knuckles were chunks of stone.

Cassidy said, "You're a slob, Haney. You're a cheap slob."

"Now, Jim, we don't want no trouble."

"I do."

"Not with me, Jim. You got no legitimate complaint against me."

Cassidy smiled just a little. "Let's just say I don't like you. And tonight I especially don't like you. It bothers me to know you gave Shealy a slamming around. Shealy's my friend."

Mildred came moving in. She stood with her face close to Cassidy's face and said, "It ain't because of Shealy and you know it. You're jealous, that's all. You're just plain jealous."

"Of you?" Cassidy said. "That's a laugh."

"Is it?" she challenged. "Then let's see you laugh."

Instead of laughing he shoved his flat palm into her face and pushed hard and Mildred went staggering back, lost her balance and hit the floor. She landed with a loud bump, sat there showing her teeth and hissing as she said, "All right, Haney. Get him for that. Don't let him do that to me."

Kenrick's face assumed a trapped expression. But he was deadly serious in his want for Mildred, and it had grown to such proportions that it far exceeded anything else in his mind. He knew he had to have Mildred and this might be the way to win her. Kenrick pulled the weight of his paunch up into his chest and moved toward Cassidy and swung with all his strength.

Cassidy wasn't fast enough. It was a roundhouse right hand and it caught him full on the jaw. He went flying back and collided with a table and was bent back over it as Kenrick came at him again. Kenrick grabbed his legs and heaved him across the top of the table, then circled the table to kick him in the ribs and aim another kick. Cassidy rolled away, leaped up and tried to defend himself and couldn't do it. Kenrick smashed his mouth with a straight left, then blasted another left to the nose, and a right to the head. And Cassidy went down again.

It was a fine, delicious moment for Kenrick. He was certain he had finished Cassidy, and he started to turn away. But from the corner of his eye he saw Cassidy getting up.

"Don't be foolish, Jim," he said. "You'll wind up in an ambulance."

Cassidy collected spit and blood between his teeth and spat it in Kenrick's face. He came lunging at Kenrick,

30

speared Kenrick with a straight left to the mouth, followed with a right that hit Kenrick on the temple. Kenrick clutched at him, grabbed him, got both arms around his middle and squeezed, and they went to the floor. They rolled across the floor, Kenrick increasing his advantage with all the power in his heavy arms, squeezing the air from Cassidy, squeezing and squeezing until Cassidy's pain was dark gray and then thick black and it felt like it was the end of everything.

Kenrick smiled at him and said, "You done?"

Cassidy began a nod that couldn't be completed because his head butted against Kenrick's chin. Kenrick let out a noise that mixed a groan with a sigh, and the arms fell away from Cassidy's middle. And Cassidy was up, saw Kenrick getting up, and allowed Kenrick to walk into a straight left to the eye. It set Kenrick, it straightened him, and Cassidy threw a booming overhand right that came down like a sledge hammer against Kenrick's jaw.

Kenrick sailed back and landed flat. His eyes were closed and he was unconscious. Cassidy looked at him, took another look to make sure, grinned down at him, then cruised gently into a soft white mist and fell on top of him.

Chapter Four

They were splashing water in Cassidy's face. They had him in one of the unfurnished rooms above the bar. As he opened his eyes he saw them peering at him anxiously. He grinned and tried to sit up. Shealy told him to take it easy. He said he wanted a drink and Spann handed him a bottle. He took a long drink. In the midst of it, he saw Mildred. He looked straight at her as he finished the drink. Then he pulled himself up from the floor and moved toward Mildred.

He said, "You get the hell out of here."

"I'm taking you home."

"Home?" He spoke in low tones. "Who said I had a home?"

31

"Come on," she said, and she reached to take his arm. "Let's go."

He pushed her hand away. "Keep away from me. I mean it."

"All right," she said. "Any way you want it."

She turned and walked out, and he heard Shealy saying, "That was wrong, Cassidy. That wasn't fair."

He looked at Shealy. "You're not in it."

"I'm just saying it wasn't fair. She tried to meet you halfway."

"Tell me about it next week." He turned away from Shealy and put a finger to his mouth and it came away bloody. He was starting to feel the pain of his bruises. To no one in particular he said, "Where's my friend Haney?"

Spann laughed lightly. "They took him to a doctor."

Cassidy felt the side of his jaw. "You know," he said, "that fat bastard put up a good fight."

They went downstairs to the bar. Cassidy said he could stand another drink.

Shealy shook his head. "I think you better call it a night. We'll take you home."

"I said I wasn't going home." He gestured to Lundy and the old man stared at him, looked past him at Shealy, who went on shaking his head. Cassidy turned and looked at Shealy and said, "Who made you my uncle?"

"I'm just your friend."

"Then do me a favor," Cassidy said. "Get out of my hair."

"It's a pity," Shealy said.

"What's a pity?"

"You're blindfolded," Shealy said. "You're just not able to see."

Cassidy waved wearily and turned his back to the white-haired man. Behind the bar Lundy was pouring a drink for Cassidy. It made no difference to Lundy that Cassidy had raised hell in his place tonight. They were always raising hell in Lundy's Place. Fights and near riots were part of the trade, and Lundy's refusal to interfere was one of the traits that made him especially popular along the water front. Another trait that made him popular was his willingness to serve them drinks long after they were loaded with it. He

32

even had a back room reserved for after-curfew drinking. Now, as he served Cassidy, all he wanted from Cassidy was thirty cents for the shot of rye.

Cassidy had three drinks and decided to buy drinks for everyone. As he turned to invite the house to drink with him, he saw that they had all gone except a single customer who sat in a far corner of the room.

She sat there with an empty glass in front of her. She was looking at the glass as though it were the page of a book and she were reading a story. Cassidy moved toward her, trying to remember her name. Dorothy, or something. Or Dora. He wondered if he was too drunk to talk to her.

He stood weaving, looking at the center of the table, which seemed to spin. "I can't remember your name."

"Doris."

"Yeah, that's right."

"Sit down," she said, smiling kindly but impersonally.

"If I sit, I'll fall asleep."

"You look tired," Doris said.

"I'm drunk."

"So am I."

Cassidy frowned at her. "You don't look drunk."

"I'm very drunk. I always know when I'm very drunk."

"That's bad," Cassidy said. "That means you're a bad case."

Doris nodded. "Yes, I'm a very sick person. They tell me I'm drinking myself to death."

Cassidy reached for a chair, knocked it over, had trouble getting it upright, and finally planted himself in it. "I never seen you here before," he said. "Where you from?"

"Nebraska." She slowly raised her hand and pointed a finger at him. "You've had an accident. Your face is all cut up."

"Well, for Christ's sake. Where were you? Didn't you see what happened?"

"I heard some excitement," Doris said.

"Didn't you see it? Didn't you see the fight?"

She lowered her head and looked at the empty glass. Cassidy stared at her.

After long moments of quiet he said, "I don't know how to figure you."

Doris smiled sadly. "I'm easy to figure. I'm just a sick person, that's all. The only thing I want to do is drink."

"How old are you?"

"Twenty-seven."

Cassidy tried to fold his arms across his chest, but couldn't get them adjusted. He let them fall to the sides of the chair. He leaned forward a little and said, "You're very young, you know that? You're just a girl. A tiny girl. I bet you don't weigh no more than ninety."

"Ninety-five."

"There," he said, trying to think of what he was saying, trying to drill his way through the wall of his drunkenness. "You're young and you're little and it's a shame."

"What's a shame?"

"Drinking. You shouldn't drink like that." He raised his hand slowly and tried to form it into a fist so he could hit it on the table. His hand fell limply against the table and he said, "You want a drink?"

Doris nodded.

Cassidy searched the room for Lundy but the barman was not in sight. He figured Lundy was in the back room and he got up from the table, called Lundy's name, took a few steps and fell on his knees.

"Oh, Jesus," he said. "I feel rotten."

He felt her hands on his arms, knew she was trying to lift him from the floor. He tried to help her but his knees gave way again and she fell with him. They sat there on the floor and looked at each other. She reached out and took his hand and used him as a support to pick herself up from the floor. Then she tried to lift him and now, very slowly, they made it, rising like battered, choked animals, dazed in a forest of smoke. His arm was flung over her shoulder and she was bent under his weight as they moved across the room toward the door leading to the street.

They came out on the street in the quiet and dark of half-past two in the morning, with a mist flowing toward them from the river. There were lights and noises on some of the piers, and there was some activity with barges out in the middle of the river. On the river side of Dock Street a policeman looked at them, frowned at them, took a few steps

34

toward them, and then decided they were just a couple of drunks and the hell with them.

The pavement ended and they advanced across the cobblestones with a seriousness that made each forward step a problem to be studied, to be handled carefully and very slowly. It was extremely important that they stay on their feet, that they hold onto consciousness and make their way across the street. To them it had the same importance as a salmon's fight for the upstream haven. The same importance as the grim journey of an injured panther seeking water. Their bodies, poisoned and weakened with alcohol, were chunks of animal substance devoid of thought and emotion and moving, moving, merely trying to survive a horrible voyage from one side of the street to the other.

In the middle of the street they fell again and Cassidy managed to grab her before her head hit the cobblestones. Some light from a street lamp drifted onto her face and he saw that she was expressionless. The look in her eyes was the lost dead look far beyond caring, beyond the inclination to care.

He struggled with her, and again they were on their feet. They moved in a path that had no direction, moving off to the side, then back again, circling and retreating and advancing and finally arriving at the other side of the street and leaning heavily against the street lamp.

As they rested there the damp air coming from the river revived them a little and they were able to look at each other with recognition.

"What I need," Cassidy said, "is just one more drink."

The dead look left her eyes. "Let's buy a drink."

"We'll go back to Lundy's," he said, "and we'll have another drink."

But then suddenly she shivered and he felt the tender frail body quivering against him, sensed the frenzy of her attempt to keep from falling once more. He held her upright and said, "I'm with you, Doris. It's all right."

"Guess I'll go home. Should I go home?"

He nodded. "I'll take you home."

"Can't—" she began.

"Can't what?"

"Can't remember the address."

35

"Try to remember. If we hang around here, they'll come with the wagon and we'll end up in the jug."

Doris gazed at the glowing cobblestones under the street lamp. She lowered her head and put her hand to her brow. After a while she was able to remember her address.

Toward five in the morning a storm came in from the northeast, a hammering of wind and rain that attacked all of the city and seemed to center its fury on the water front. The river swirled and cut itself apart and shot vicious waves at the piers, some of the waves breaking over the lower piers and sending platoons of foam halfway across Dock Street. The cascade of rain was a blinding onslaught, like billions of rivets coming down. In the stalls along Dock Street and Front Street and in the truck terminals farther up along Delaware Avenue they stopped all activity and ran for shelter and knew there'd be no work today.

The crash of rain awakened Cassidy and he sat up and instantly realized he had been sleeping on a floor. He wondered what he was doing on the floor. Then he decided it didn't matter where he was, because he couldn't possibly feel any worse. His head felt as though someone who didn't like him had inserted tubes through his eyeballs and into his brain and sent hot metal through the tubes. His stomach seemed to have fallen to his knees. Every nerve cell in his body had a separate kind of agony. He told himself he was certainly a sad case. He rolled over on his side and went back to sleep.

Around half-past ten he woke again and heard the rain. It was quite dark in the room and yet there was enough light for him to see his surroundings. He rubbed his eyes and wondered what in God's name he was doing in a room he had never seen before. Then, as he lifted himself from the floor, he saw Doris sleeping in the bed. And he remembered how she had passed out on one of the side streets, how he had carried her here, put her in the bed, and then passed out himself.

He took another look at the room. It was very small and shabby, but it smelled clean and there was a door that gave way to a bathroom and another door leading into a tiny kitchen. He decided what he needed first was the bathroom. When he came out he felt a little better. There was a pack of cigarettes and a book of matches on the dresser and he helped himself to a smoke and walked into the kitchen, thinking of hot coffee.

There was a clock in the kitchen and as he looked at the dial he let out a groan, knowing it was too late to report for work. But then he realized it was Sunday. Not only that, it was storming outside to such an extent that the streets and roads were in no condition for driving. He looked out the kitchen window and it was like gazing through the porthole of a submerged ship. The sound of the rain was a cannonade aiming in all directions and he told himself it was a fine day to be inside.

At the kitchen table he sat placidly, enjoying the cigarette, waiting for the coffee to boil. He noticed some books on a shelf near the stove, and he got up and took a look at the titles. As he read the titles he bit gently at his lower lip. The books were works of instruction on the science of self-cure of the alcohol habit. He opened one of them and noticed she had made some notes in the margins. There was a certain intelligence apparent in the handwriting, a purposefulness amounting to frantic effort. But toward the middle chapters the notes ended, and in the final chapters the pages looked untouched.

The coffee boiled and he poured himself a cup, winced as the hot black liquid seared his mouth. But it made him feel good inside and he kept drinking it down and poured a second cup. Now he was feeling a lot better and the thick metallic weight in his head was going away. As he started the third cup, he heard her moving around in the bedroom. Then he heard the bathroom door closing and the sound of a faucet running.

It was a good sound. It was a strong, positive sound, the noise of a bathtub faucet, and she probably did that every morning. It was nice to know that she bathed every day. Most of them here along the water front used cheap cologne and put various creams in their armpits but they seldom bathed.

37

He lit another cigarette and had more coffee. He sat there listening to the mingled sounds of the storm outside and the splashing in the bathroom. Within him there was a certain sense of pleasant expectancy that had nothing to do with the senses, a gently sheltered and completely relaxed feeling. It was just nice to be here. And the coffee and tobacco tasted fine.

Then he heard the bathroom door opening and her footsteps moving toward the kitchen. He smiled a good-morning smile at her as she entered the kitchen. Her hair was brushed and she wore a clean dress, a pale-yellow cotton of simple design.

She returned his smile and said, "How do you feel?"

He nodded. "Recovering."

"I took a cold bath. It always does something for me." She moved toward the stove and poured herself a cup of coffee and brought it to the table. She lifted the cup, frowned at it, put it down and looked at Cassidy. She said, "Where did you sleep?"

"On the floor." He said it with emphasis. He wanted to be sure she didn't get the wrong idea.

But then he realized she hadn't been thinking of that, because the concern in her eyes was only for his comfort. She said, "You must be stiff as a board. I guess you didn't get much sleep."

"I was out like a light."

The concern remained in her eyes. "You sure you feel all right now?"

"I'm doing fine."

She turned her attention to the coffee. After a few sips, she said, "Would you like a drink?"

"Hell, no," Cassidy said. "Don't even mention the word."

"Would you mind if I had one?"

He was about to say he didn't mind, of course he didn't mind, and why should he mind? But his lips were somewhat stiff, and his eyes were solemn, kind of paternal. And he said, "Do you really need it?"

"Badly."

He smiled with tender pleading. "Try to get past it."

"I can't. I really can't get past it. I need it to pick me up."

He inclined his head, studying her. "How long have you been on it this time?"

"I don't know," she said. "I never count the days."

"You mean the weeks," Cassidy said. He sighed wearily. "All right, go ahead. If I tied you up with rope, I couldn't stop you."

She leaned back a little and regarded him with a childlike seriousness. "Why should you want to stop me?"

He opened his mouth to reply and discovered he had no adequate answer. He looked at the floor. He heard her rising from the table and going into the bedroom. Thinking about what was taking place in the bedroom, he visualized her deliberate approach to the bottle, the terrible calm and quiet as she lifted the bottle, the dreadful companionship between the bottle and herself. He could see the bottle rising to her lips, and then her lips meeting the lips of the bottle, as though the bottle were something alive, making love to her.

A shudder streaked through Cassidy, and in the deep ridges of his mind he saw the bottle as a loathsome, grotesque creature that had lured Doris and captured her and pleasured itself with her, draining the sweet life from her body as it poured its rottenness into her. He saw the bottle as something poisonous and altogether hateful, and Doris completely helpless in its grasp.

Then his mind was dizzy and his eyes were blank as he rose slowly from the table, and for a moment he just stood there, not at all sure of what he meant to do. But as he started toward the bedroom there was a grimness in his stride, and as he entered the bedroom the grimness increased, and he moved toward Doris, who stood facing the window, her head tilted back, the bottle at her lips.

Cassidy snatched at the bottle, caught hold of it and held it high above his head, and then, with all the power in his arm, he heaved it to the floor. It cracked and burst and the glass and whisky made a silver-amber spray.

It was quiet and he was looking at her and she was looking at the broken glass on the floor. The quiet lasted for the better part of a minute.

Finally she looked at Cassidy and said, "I can't understand why you did that."

"To help you."

"Why should you want to help me?"

He moved toward the window and gazed out at the blinding rain. "I don't know. I'm trying to figure it out."

He heard her saying, "You can't help me. There isn't anything you can do."

The rain slashed against the window. It glimmered and whirled going down along a tenement wall across the alley. Cassidy wanted to speak but he had no specific idea to express. He wondered vaguely if it would rain all day.

He heard Doris saying, "Nothing you can do. Nothing at all."

Cassidy stared through the window and through a gap in the tenement walls across the alley. The gap extended toward Dock Street and beyond the street and he saw the rain-blackened sky above the river.

And he heard her saying, "Three years. I've been on it three years. In Nebraska I was married and I had children. We had a little farm. A few acres. I didn't like the farm. I cared for him with all my heart but I hated the farm. At night I couldn't sleep and I would read a lot and smoke in bed. He said it was dangerous to smoke in bed."

Cassidy turned very slowly. He saw she was alone with herself now, talking aloud to herself.

She said, "Maybe I did it purposely. I don't know. If God in heaven would only tell me I didn't do it purposely—" She lifted her fingers to her lips, as though she was trying to close her lips, trying to stop the words from coming out. But her lips moved. "—not to know whether I did it purposely. Not to know. Only know how much I hated the farm. I'd never lived on a farm. I couldn't get used to it. And that night when I smoked in bed and fell asleep. And when I woke up a man was carrying me. I saw all the people. I saw the house on fire. I looked for my husband and children but I couldn't see them. How could I see them when they were in the house? All I could see was the house burning down."

Then her eyes were closed and he knew she was seeing it again.

And she said, "They were very nice to me. My family and all my friends. But that didn't help. That made it worse. One night I cut my wrists. Another time I tried to jump out of a hospital window. And after that happened they gave me a drink. It was the first time I'd ever tasted liquor. It tasted good. Had a burning taste. Burning."

She sat down on the edge of the bed and stared at the floor.

Cassidy began to walk back and forth. He had his hands behind his back and he was twisting and squeezing his fingers.

He was thinking about all of them. All the victims of the drink habit. The extent to which they drank and their reasons for the drinking. Then he looked at Doris. And all the others were gone from his mind. He saw the pure and kind and delicate sweetness of Doris, the innocence of Doris, the soft and mild, yet somehow powerful, glow of goodness that she radiated. He felt the kind of pain that one feels when seeing a crippled child. And all at once he felt an enormous desire to help Doris.

And yet he didn't know what to do. He didn't know how to begin. He saw her sitting there on the edge of the bed, her tiny white hands resting limply in her lap, her shoulders drooped in the attitude of someone lost in a labyrinth.

He spoke her name and she raised her head and gazed at him. There was a plaintive pleading in her eyes. For a split instant he was aware that she was pleading for another bottle. But he didn't want to know that. He didn't want to think about it.

He stayed with it only long enough to mutter, "You don't need it."

And as he said that, he knew what she needed. What he himself had needed and found in the soft-glowing purity of her presence. He moved toward her. His smile was tender. He took her hand, and there was nothing physical in the contact. It was like a gentle murmur as he lifted her hand to his lips and kissed the tips of her fingers. She was staring at him with a sort of passive waiting, but her eyes gradually widened in wonderment as he put his arms around her.

"You're good, Doris," he said. "You're so good."

She stared very widely and at first there was only the astonishment of discovering she was in his arms. But then she felt the warm comfort of his chest, the assurance of his nearness, the pure tenderness she could see in his eyes and feel in his touch. And there was a sense of resting, of being pillowed and sheltered and sweetly, softly protected. Without speaking, just by looking at him, she was able to communicate her feeling to Cassidy and he smiled at her and held her more closely.

Then he raised her head slightly and lowered his head and saw her pale gold hair drifting past, her gray eyes slowly closing in the placid happiness of knowing the truth and kindness of this moment. Knowing the meaning of the moment. As his lips came nearer. As his lips came softly nearer and then were soft upon her lips and remained there as her arms encircled his wide shoulders, her palms pressing against the thick power of his shoulder muscles.

It seemed that without moving they were floating backward and onto the bed so that they were prone on the bed, their lips still softly locked, their flesh warming with the sort warmth of allowing it to happen as it was happening.

And warmer. And still warmer. The good warmth. A cherished warmth, Cassidy told himself. Because it was right. Because it had nothing to do with lust. It was desire, but mostly of the spirit, and the bodily feeling was only what the spirit felt.

It was physical because it was expressed in physical terms. But the tenderness was far greater than the passion. She bit her lips with embarrassment and mutely tried to tell him she was ashamed of her nakedness, and he leaned down and kissed her shame away. She moved her mouth against his mouth, as though silently saying, I'm grateful, I'm grateful, and now I'm not ashamed, I'm only glad, just glad, and let it happen.

He raised his head and looked at her and saw the tiny breasts, the fragility of her limbs, the babylike smoothness of her skin. It was all soft and pale and delicate, like a blending of pale flower petals. The curves of her body were mild, scarcely apparent, just barely suggested, and she was so thin, so pitifully thin. And yet, that in itself was a stimulus for his need to caress her, to give her something of his strength.

Then, as he put his hand on her breast, he knew the yearning was very great and it was her way of telling him to please let it happen now. He knew he was ready for it to happen, he was intensely glad it was going to happen. And now as it began to happen it was with a soft, very soft, almost gentle pressure. Because she was dainty and he mustn't hurt her. Not the slightest hurt or discomfort, not the slightest suggestion of conquest. Because it was entirely aside from conquest. It was giving, the wondrous untainted giving, and now as she received it she sighed. She sighed again. And again, and again, and again.

He heard the sigh. That was all he heard. Beyond the wall of the room the storm stampeded upon the streets of the water front, and the raging sound of it came lunging at Cassidy's ears. But all he heard was the gentle sighing of Doris.

Late in the afternoon the rainstorm reached an intensity that blackened the sky and caused the city to cringe under the booming downpour. Along the water front the ships seemed to press themselves against the docks, as though trying to seek cover. Through the window looking out upon the tenement alley, Cassidy could see only the dark, shimmering blur of the neighboring walls. He smiled at the rain and told it to go on raining. He was content to lie here on the bed and watch the rain coming down, liking the angry sound of it, sort of a frustrated sound because it couldn't get anywhere near him.

Doris was in the kitchen. She had suggested that they have something to eat and she insisted on preparing the dinner herself. She promised Cassidy it would be a very nice dinner.

Cassidy rolled himself off the bed and went into the bathroom. He looked in the mirror and decided to improve his appearance for the dinner with Doris. In the medicine cabinet he found a small curved razor, designed for women. At first he had some trouble with it, but gradually scraped it against his face until the bristles were gone. Then he filled the bathtub with lukewarm water

43

and lowered himself into it and sat there for a while. He told himself he had been a long time away from anything approaching a home.

It seemed altogether natural to him that he should use Doris' comb and her bottle of skin freshener to freeze away the razor nicks on his face. It seemed unbelievable that until last night he had never known there was such a person as Doris.

Then, as he came into the bedroom and started to dress, it occurred to him that he must have known. Somehow he must have known, he must have been waiting for the arrival of Doris in his life. He told himself he had been waiting and hoping, and aching with the hope. And now it had taken place. It was actual. She was right there in the kitchen, fixing him a dinner.

He heard Doris calling that dinner was ready, and he went into the kitchen and saw the table neatly arranged, and smelled the nice smell of a really good dinner. There was a chicken stew and she had made biscuits and opened a jar of olives. She stood there at the stove, smiling meekly and saying, "I hope it tastes good."

Cassidy moved toward her. He put his arms around her and said, "You knew I was hungry and you came in here and fixed a dinner for me."

She didn't know how to respond. She shrugged uncertainly and said, "Well, sure, Jim. Why not?"

"You know what that means to me?"

Doris lowered her head bashfully.

He put his hand under her chin and gently lifted her head. He said, "It means a hell of a lot. It means more than I can tell you."

She brought her fingertips to his shoulders. She looked up at him and her eyes were large with wonder. Her lips barely moved as she said, "Listen to it raining."

"Doris—"

"Listen," she said. "Listen to the rain."

"I want you, Doris."

"Me?" She said it mechanically.

"I want you," he said. "I want to be with you. Here. I want it to go on like this. You and me."

"Jim," she murmured, and she looked at the floor. "What can I say?"

"Say it's all right."

She went on looking at the floor. "Sure it's all right. It's—it's dandy."

"But it isn't dandy, is it? You think it's all wrong."

She raised her hand to the side of her head, pressed her fingers against her temple. "Please, Jim. Please bear with me. I'm trying to think."

"About what? What's bothering you?"

She started to turn away. He pulled her back and she said, "It isn't fair. You have a wife."

He held onto her arms. "Listen, Doris. Just look at me and listen and let me tell you something. I ain't been living with a wife. Married to her, sure, but she ain't a wife. I'll tell you what she is. She's a tramp. A no-good tramp. And I'm finished with her. You hear? I'm finished, I'll never go back. I want to stay here with you."

Doris leaned her head against his chest. She didn't say anything.

"From now on," Cassidy said, "you're my woman."

"Yes," she breathed. "I'm your woman."

"That's right," he told her. "That's settled. Now let's sit down and have ourselves a meal."

Chapter Five

During the night an abrupt shifting of the wind sent the storm clouds away from the city, and in the morning the streets were dry. Cassidy was due at the depot at nine, and as he ate a quick breakfast of coffee and toast he complained to Doris about the way the company treated its drivers. He said the company had one hell of a crust, expecting the drivers to come in two hours before the first run. He said the company had one hell of a crust, expecting the drivers to make mechanical repairs on the busses and clean the depot and do all sorts of odd jobs that had nothing to do with driving a bus. But his complaint wasn't serious. It was typical Monday-morning griping. After he had said it, and Doris had nodded in agreement with his point of view, he completely forgot about it, and he was ready to start off for a day's work.

At the door, just before he left, he asked her what her plans were for the day. She groped for an adequate answer, and he said he didn't care what she did as long as she stayed away from the bottle and away from Lundy's Place. She promised to follow his orders. She said it might be worth while for her to take a walk on Market Street, and perhaps she might land a job behind the counter in one of the department stores. Cassidy told her not to worry about getting a job. He said that from here on she wouldn't have to worry about anything. He kissed her, and as he backed away from the door, he blew her a kiss.

On his way to the trolley line on Arch Street, he passed the ship chandlery where Shealy worked. He caught a glimpse of the white hair through the plate-glass window, and decided to go in and say good morning to Shealy. For some unknown reason he was anxious to have a chat with Shealy, although he was nowhere near an idea as to what the topic would be.

Shealy was busy with a new stock of seamen's sweaters and working pants. He was up on a ladder, arranging the merchandise on a top shelf. As the sound of Cassidy's voice he started down immediately, without looking at Cassidy. He came out from behind the counter and worriedly put his hands on Cassidy's shoulders.

"For Christ's sake," he said to Cassidy, "where you been? All day yesterday I waited in Lundy's. Figured at least you'd show up to tell me what happened."

Cassidy shrugged. "Nothing happened."

Shealy backed away to get a better perspective of Cassidy's appearance. "We know you didn't go home. We asked Mildred and she said you didn't show."

Cassidy turned away and moved toward one of the side counters and looked down at a display of sunglasses. He put his hands on the edge of the counter and leaned low over it and said, "I was with Doris."

Then he waited, and after some moments he heard Shealy saying, "It sums up. I should have known it sums up."

Cassidy turned. He looked at Shealy. He said quietly, "What's wrong with you?"

Shealy did not reply. He was sending his eyes through Cassidy's eyes and trying to see the core of Cassidy's mind.

"All right," Cassidy said. "Let's hear the sad music."

The white-haired man folded his arms and gazed past Cassidy's shoulder and said, "Leave her alone, Jim."

"For what good reason?"

"She's helpless. She's a sick girl."

"I know that," Cassidy said. "That's why I won't leave her alone. That's why I'm staying with her." He hadn't meant to state his complete plans, but now, as though Shealy was challenging him, he met the challenge and said bluntly, "I won't be going back to Mildred. I'll never be with Mildred again. From now on you'll find me living with Doris."

Shealy moved toward the ladder and gazed up at the top shelf where the sweaters and working pants were stacked. His eyes were appraising and finally he seemed to be satisfied with the arrangement. But he went on looking up there at the merchandise as he said, "Why not take it further than that? If you're out to help all the poor creatures of the world, why don't you found a mission?"

"You go to hell," Cassidy said. He started toward the door.

"Wait, Jim."

"Wait nothing. I come in to say good morning and you give me the needles."

"You didn't come in to say good morning." Shealy was with him at the door and not allowing him to open it. "You come in because you want assurance. You want me to tell you that you're doing right."

"You? I need you to tell me?" Cassidy tried a sarcastic smile. All that showed was a scowl as he said, "What makes you so important?"

"The fact that I'm out of it," Shealy replied. "Entirely out of the show. Just a one-man audience, sitting in the balcony. That gives me a full view. I can see it from every angle."

Cassidy grimaced impatiently. "Quit the syrup, will you? Talk plain."

"All right, Jim. I'll make it as plain as I can. I'm just a

worn-out rumhead, slowly rotting away. But there's one thing left alive in me, one thing working and holding me in line. That's my brains. It's my brains and only my brains telling you to keep away from Doris."

Here we go, Cassidy said to the wall. "Now it starts with the preaching."

"Me preach?" And Shealy laughed. "Not me, Jim. Anyone but me. I lost my sense of moral values a long time ago. The credo I hold today is based on simple arithmetic, nothing more. We can all survive and get along if we can just add one and one and get two."

"What's that got to do with me and Doris?"

"If you don't leave her alone," Shealy said, "she won't survive."

Cassidy took a backward step. He narrowed his eyes. "Come on, Shealy, come on downstairs. Come out of the clouds."

Shealy folded his arms again as he leaned back against the counter. "Jim," he said, "before last night I'd never seen that girl. But I sat there at the table and I watched her take one drink. And that told me everything. Doris has only one need, and that's whisky."

Cassidy took a deep breath. He aimed a kick at the floor and said, "You ought to rent yourself an office. Put up a sign. My name is Doctor Shealy and for five bucks a visit I'll teach you how to louse up your life."

"I can't teach anybody anything," Shealy said. "All I can do is show you what's in front of your face." He took hold of Cassidy's arm and led him to the plate-glass window. Beyond the window the cobbled street was a narrow, dust-covered twisting path bordered with the leaning, decayed walls of tenements. The air was gray with the gaseous grime of the water front.

"There it is," Shealy said. "There's your life. My life. Nobody dragged us down here. We dragged ourselves. Wanting it. Knowing it was just what we wanted and we'd be comfortable. Like pigs who go for the mud, because there's no bumps, it's soft—"

"It's rotten," Cassidy said. "It's filth. I've had enough of it. I'm getting out."

48

Shealy sighed. "The dreams again." He shook his head with a kind of sorrow. "I've been here eighteen years and I've heard thousands of dreams. And they've all been the same. I'm getting out. I'm climbing up. I'm taking her by the hand and we'll find the road together. The shining road that aims upward."

Cassidy waved wearily and said, "What's the use? I won't get anywhere talking to you."

He turned his back to Shealy, went to the door, opened it and walked out. He was annoyed with himself for having visited Shealy and allowing the older man to assume the role of counselor. But to the same extent he was gratified to know he had completely rejected Shealy's point of view. He told himself he would continue to reject that kind of thinking, hurdle it and run from it and stay away from it. In that connection, it might be a good idea to stay away from Shealy. And certainly he was going to stay away from Lundy's Place.

It was like placing his plans on the edge of a spring board, letting them bounce a little, bracing them and then letting them go. They were good plans, he knew, and they soared in his mind. He saw Doris and himself packing the bags and moving away from the gray stagnation of the water front. Going somewhere uptown to one of those low-rent housing projects where each little house had a patch of green in front. He'd ask the bus people for a raise and he knew they wouldn't say no. He was certainly due for a raise and right about now he more or less had them against a wall. The drivers were always getting sore and quitting and lately they'd lost two good drivers and he was the only one left who could really be depended upon. It might go up as high as sixty a week and that was plenty, that was all right.

The only complication was the fact that Mildred might make trouble. But the chances were he could buy Mildred off, maybe pay her off in installments until the divorce was over and done with. Come to think of it, he'd be able to evade the financial angle entirely if Haney Kenrick footed the bill. And the chances were Haney would be only too eager to do that.

He came to the end of the narrow side street leading into Front Street, started up Front toward Arch. A few blocks ahead the street was crammed with early-morning trucking activity, but down here there was an emptiness and a quiet, a jagged broken line of neglected real estate and condemned houses. A cat came racing after a rat from underneath a busted fence and Cassidy stopped for a moment to watch the chase. The rat was almost as large as its pursuer. It was very anxious that it shouldn't be caught, but on the other side of the street it became confused and found itself wedged in between piles of bricks. The cat came in, rushing in toward it, and it hunched itself against the wall, braced itself to leap at the rat.

That was as much as Cassidy saw, because just then he sensed something whizzing toward him, as though suddenly the air near his head was compressed and heavy. Mechanically he moved his head just a little, heard the swish and hiss and saw the rectangular shape sailing past. He saw the brick crashing against the wall of a deserted warehouse and in the same instant he pivoted to see who had thrown the brick.

He saw Haney Kenrick trying to dart into an alleyway. His initial impulse was to chase after Haney and resume the battle. The action of Saturday night should have terminated the argument, but apparently Haney felt the need of continued rebuttal. Cassidy took a few steps toward the alleyway and then stopped short, shrugged and decided it wasn't worth the effort. Anyway, Haney must know that he had been seen and it was a hundred to one he wouldn't try anything like that again.

Cassidy continued toward Arch Street. Arriving at Arch, he crossed the street going east toward Second, where people on the corner were waiting for the trolley. The sun was up very full and hot and he knew it would be a scorcher today. Already he could feel the pressure of the sun and he could see the blaze of it bouncing off the store windows along Arch Street. He told himself it would be a damn sensible idea to check the rear tires of the bus. Last week another driver had gone out on a hot day and the burning road had rubbed its way through and there was a blowout.

50

Almost a bad accident, and if the bus had turned over it would have been too bad. Cassidy solemnly repeated it to himself. On a high-Fahrenheit day such as this, it was very important to check the tires. He was crossing First Street and thinking about the tires and then someone called his name.

It was Mildred's voice. He saw her standing there on the other side of Arch. She had her hands on her hips. She was wearing a blouse and skirt and high-heeled shoes. Some men were passing by and a few of them sneaked a glance backward. Others were more brazen and stopped for a moment to have themselves a look. She was a big, gorgeous ornament standing there on the corner of First Street and Arch.

"Cassidy," she called, and her voice was rich and full, a projectile of sound, bursting against the quiet drone of the early morning, "Come here. I want to talk to you."

He didn't move. He told himself he'd talk with her when he felt good and ready.

"You hear me?" Mildred called. "Come on over here."

Cassidy shrugged and decided he might as well have it out with her now and get it over with. He advised himself to take it very easy and no matter what she said, no matter What names she called him, he mustn't lose his temper. Be cold, he said to himself. Just be ice-cold.

He crossed the street and came up to her and said, "What's on your mind?"

"I've been waiting here for you."

"So?"

She leaned her weight on one hip. "I want to know where you been."

"Call up information."

Her lower lip jutted and she said, "Now, listen, bastard—"

"We're in public," he said.

"—— the public."

"All right, then," he said. "Let's put it this way. It's too early in the morning."

"Not for me it ain't," Mildred said. "It's never too early for me."

She turned her head and looked around, and he knew

she was searching for a milk bottle or any kind of a bottle, any kind of heavy missile.

"That's over with," he said.

She blinked a few times. "What's over with?"

"The fighting. The hell-raising. Everything."

She stared at him. The finality was there on his face but she didn't believe it. Her lips curled and she said, "Look at him there, all quiet and respectable. Who took you to church?"

"It wasn't church."

"What was it?"

He didn't say anything.

Mildred took a step toward him. "You think you're smart, don't you? You think you're putting something over. Well, let me tell you a thing or two. I don't get fooled easy. I got good eyes and I know what's happening."

She prodded a finger against his chest, then shoved both hands at his chest, started to shove again but he grabbed her wrists and said, "Lay off. I'm warning you, lay off."

"Let go my hands."

"So you can swing at me?"

"I said let go." She tried to twist away. "I'll tear your eyes out. I'll rip your face apart—"

"No, you won't." The steady deadly calm of it caused her to stop struggling, and as he released her wrists she didn't move. He said, "I'll say it once and you'll hear it and that's all. We're washed up."

"Listen, Cassidy—"

"No. I'm talking. Didn't you hear? I said we're washed up."

"You mean you're moving out?"

"That's the general idea. When I get off work today I'm coming back to the flat and packing up."

She snapped her fingers. "Just like that?"

He nodded. "Like that."

For a stretched moment she didn't say anything. She just looked at him. Then she said quietly, "You'll be back."

"You think so? Sit there and wait."

She let that pass. She said, "What do you want, Cassidy? You want to see a performance? I should break down in

52

tears? I should beg you to stay? I should get down on my knees? Why, you, you—" She raised her fist, held it in front of him for a moment, then let it drop.

He turned and started to walk away from her. She came after him, grabbed him and twisted him around.

"Lay off," he said. "I said it's final. It can't be patched up."

"Damn you," she seethed. "Did I say I want it patched up? All I want is—"

"What? What?"

"I want you to come out with it. Who is it?"

"That ain't the point."

"You're a liar." Her arm flashed and she smacked him full across the face. "You're a no-good liar." She smacked him again and with her other hand she grabbed his shirt and held him there and smacked him a third time. "You rotten bastard," she shrieked.

He rubbed the side of his face. He muttered, "People are looking."

"Let them look," Mildred yelled. "Let them get a good look." She glared at the people who were standing around and looking. "To hell with you," she said to them.

A stout middle-aged woman said, "It's shameful. It's a disgrace."

"Go chase yourself," Mildred told the woman. Then she turned to Cassidy and shouted, "Sure, that's me. I'm a bum. I got no manners, I got no breeding. I'm just a broad, a skirt. But still I got privileges. I know I got certain privileges." She lunged at Cassidy and with both hands she grabbed thick locks of his hair, forcing his head back and screaming, "I got a right to know. And you're gonna tell me. Who's the woman?"

Cassidy took hold of her arms and freed himself. He stepped back and said, "All right. Her name is Doris."

"Doris?" She stared off to one side. "Doris?" Then her stare aimed at Cassidy. "That nothing? That skinny little drunk?" Her stare became dazed and she said, "Jesus Christ, is that who it is? Is that my competition?"

Cassidy begged himself not to hit her. He knew if he hit her now he would do very serious damage. He bit his lip

53

hard and then he said, "I've made up my mind I want to marry Doris. Will you go get a divorce?"

Mildred went on staring at him.

He said, "Will you get a divorce? Answer me."

She answered him. She leaned toward him and her spit splashed against his face. As the saliva dripped down his cheek, he saw her turning and walking away. He heard the people murmuring and some of them laughing and one of the men said, "Wow!"

Chapter Six

In the trolley sliding along the hot tracks going toward the bus depot, he sat staring at the floor and feeling sort of puzzled and wondering why he was puzzled. The thing with Mildred was settled and it had happened as he should have expected it would happen. He certainly hadn't expected her to take it with a sweet smile and a friendly pat on the shoulder, wishing him good luck and saying it was nice to have known him. She had reacted in typical Mildred-fashion, and he hadn't been surprised then and he couldn't understand why he was puzzled now.

Maybe it wasn't puzzlement. If not, then what was it? He asked himself if it was the blues. But it couldn't be the blues, that wouldn't make sense. He ought to be happy. He had every reason to be happy. His situation was wholesome now, he had discovered something sanitary and decent within himself, had decided to utilize it, hold onto it, make it flourish and thus construct a better life for himself and Doris.

Himself and Doris. That wasn't quite the way to put it. Turn it around. Doris and himself. That was better. That was proper. A fine word, proper. He liked the flavor of it as it repeated itself in his mind. Proper in capital letters and underlined. Proper that he had met Doris. Proper that he had seen beyond her alcoholism, had seen the basic goodness, had been drawn toward her, not lured, not teased, but drawn slowly and surely as the devout are drawn toward a shrine. And that was proper. All his thoughts, all his plans for Doris and himself were entirely proper. The trolley was approaching the bus depot and he had cleared his mind of the incident with Mildred on the street corner. He was thinking in terms of Doris and himself and how proper it was and he felt fine.

The good feeling increased as he entered the depot and saw the bus. He went into the small locker room and put on a jumper and spent the better part of an hour checking the tires, adjusting the carburetor, testing the points. He jacked up the bus and sent grease into the transmission and tightened up on the clutch. Then sliding backward underneath the bus he saw it needed new springs. He spoke to the superintendent about it, and the super complimented him on his efficiency. In the rear storage room he found a new set of springs, put them in place and came out from underneath with his face grease-blackened and his eyes quietly happy.

He washed his face and put on a clean uniform. In the waiting room a clerk was telling the passengers it was time for the morning run to Easton. They walked eagerly toward the bus and Cassidy stood at the door and helped them in. He smiled at them and they smiled back. He tipped his cap to the older ladies and heard one of them saying to her companion, "He's so polite. It's so nice when they're courteous."

He gave his passengers a perfect ride to Easton. Not too fast, not too slow, just a perfectly paced ride with time gained on the stretches of wide highway when there was not much traffic, and caution exercised along the narrow, curving road that bordered the upper Delaware. There were places where the road climbed abruptly, where it sloped acutely and called for expert driving. He demonstrated to his passengers the meaning of really expert driving. When they arrived at Easton a middle-aged man smiled at him and said, "You sure know how to run a bus. First time I ever felt safe all the way."

It was as though the man was pinning a bright ribbon on him, and he glowed with the feeling. He sensed that he was standing straighter, that his chest was somewhat expanded and his shoulders were erect. It was on the order of the moments in the long ago when he had stood beside the big four-engined plane, having flown it across an ocean, flown it surely and safely, and landed it perfectly, to stand there and watch his passengers getting off. The good solid feeling of having accomplished a piece of work and done it well.

He stepped back into the doorway of the Easton terminal and looked at his bus. The wonderful bus that he controlled, the compact assemblage of gears and bushings and wheels that gave him a job to do, that offered him the opportunity to work each day and really belong in the world. He smiled at the bus and in his eyes there was affection and gratitude.

In the afternoon it was terribly hot, too hot for April, and it was sticky, almost stifling. But he didn't feel the weather. He told himself it was a fine day. From Easton to Philadelphia, the round trip, and then to Easton once more, and the hours passed swiftly, smoothly. He sat solidly behind the wheel, and without sound he spoke tenderly to his bus.

"Now, let's take this hill—let's take it at forty—that's it, that's just right—around the curve now—easy—that's perfect—now another curve—you're clicking, kid—you're doing great—you're a damn fine bus, you're the finest thing on four wheels—"

Through the windshield he saw the springtime green of the fields and hills, bright yellow-green under the sun. A succession of wonderful pastoral aromas came flowing toward him and he smelled the honeysuckle, the violet, the tangy fragrance of mint leaves. The delicious smells of springtime in the Delaware valley. He looked at the silver glow of the river shining in the sunlight, with the bright green slopes in the background, the Jersey shore. It was the kind of view they were always trying to put on canvas, or capture with a camera. But they couldn't see it the way he saw it. He saw it in a way that put the taste of nectar in his mouth. He felt it with the soaring, surging feeling of knowing fully and surely that after all, and aside from everything, there was really something to live for.

It was like a noble contradiction against everything negative and rotten and sordid. It was the very substance of hope and quiet strength calmly denying the grime and decay of tenement walls and the cobbled streets along the Philadelphia water front. Up here along the hills and valleys the meaning of it all was forward and upward, clean and bright and serene. It proclaimed calmly, yet decisively, that indeed there were treasures to be found on this earth, treasures that demanded no payment and no effort other than the effort of seeing it and feeling it and knowing what it meant.

Cassidy looked at the fields, at the river. The placid Delaware. The same Delaware that flowed past the Philadelphia water front. Along the piers of commerce it was a filthy river and it had a stench they called "that lousy river smell." It seemed almost impossible that this was the same Delaware. It was as though the river back there was the river not only of a different place, but of a different time. As though this scene of the upper Delaware represented a forwardness of time. As though the Delaware between Philadelphia and Camden was something far back, something in the long ago, long dead.

He told himself it was really dead. As far as he was concerned it was past history, the kind of history not worth remembering. They were no longer streets but a cobbled stretch of graves where all of them were buried, and all the shouting and the curses and the sounds of thudding fists and broken glass were stifled. It was finished, it was done for, and it would be forgotten quickly. As one rides past a dead dog in the street, shudders at the sight, feels pity for an instant, and then rides on and forgets about it.

It wouldn't take him long to forget Lundy's Place. And Pauline and Spann. And Shealy and all the others. He told himself to include Mildred. All right, that was easy. Mildred was included. Of course she was included. Why not? Why the hell not? It was a downright pleasure to include Mildred. The process of forgetting Mildred would be like emerging from the clatter and roar and blinding heat of a boiler room, and finding a quiet place and clean, fresh air.

Because Mildred was only part of an interval, that was all. An interval of degradation, wherein he had voluntarily descended, viciously casting off every noble element of his

57

being. In the same way that he had gulped alcohol to punish himself, he had married Mildred in the seething, crazy desire to contaminate his spirit by wedding it with that of a vile-mouthed water-front slut. The marriage itself was a mockery, a bizarre episode that might have taken place during a masquerade. Recalling the moment of marriage, the exact moment when he had put the ring on Mildred's finger, was like recalling the vivid colors and grotesque shapes on the cover of a horror magazine. The canopy was fire and the floor was hot coals. There were bridesmaids and they wore skin-tight bright red satin, and they had horns. The bride was given in marriage by a slimy, grinning monstrosity who kept prodding the groom with a huge, three-pronged fork. The bridegroom smiled and told the slimy one to keep it up, it felt fine.

The road curved in front of the windshield and the side of a hill came up steeply and blocked Cassidy's view of the river. The hill was covered with dandelions and daisies. It was a pretty hill and then, as his eyes traveled upward along its slope, he saw the big advertising sign telling everybody to wise up and drink a certain brand of blended whisky.

At eight-forty, as Cassidy completed his final run from Easton, the sky was darkening and the moon was out full and bright. As he stepped off the trolley at First and Arch, he sensed the mildness of the night, felt the breeze that seemed to act as a cleansing agent against sticky heat. He decided it would be a swell idea to take Doris for a walk in the park.

He started toward Doris' place, thinking how nice it would be, their having dinner together. Chances were, she had cooked another fine dinner for him, but if not, he'd take her to a good restaurant and then they'd go over to Fairmount Park and walk around the fountain near the Parkway Museum. They'd walk for a while and when they got tired they'd sit on a bench and enjoy the evening breeze.

But first, before dinner, he'd fill the tub with water and get in and use plenty of soap. He sure needed a bath. Under his driver's uniform his body felt caked with sweat and grime. He enjoyed anticipating the bath and then shaving and then putting on a clean shirt—

He snapped his fingers, remembering that all his clothes and belongings were in the bedroom of the second story flat. He wondered if Mildred was there now. He told himself it didn't matter whether she was there or not. Damn it, he had a right to collect his clothes. But maybe she would start battling again, and he certainly didn't want that. His mouth tightened. If she knew what was good for her, she wouldn't start another fuss. She sure as hell better not start with him again. There were limits to what he would take from that no-good tramp. As it was, he had taken too much on the street corner this morning. If she started with him tonight, she'd wind up wearing bandages. Go on, let her start with him. Let her be there, waiting for him. Just let her start something.

He walked faster, not realizing he actually hoped she was there, wanting to start something. As he entered the tenement building, he had his fists clenched. He hurried up the dark stairway and threw open the door and lunged into the flat.

The living room was in the same disordered state. Either she had thrown another party or she hadn't moved a muscle to clean up the wreckage from three nights ago. He kicked a chair aside and walked into the bedroom and moved toward the closet. All at once he stopped to stare at an ash tray.

The ash tray rested on a table beside the bed. He looked at the cigar stub in the ash tray. Then he looked at the crumpled sheets on the bed, and one of the pillows on the floor.

Well? he asked himself. So what? What did it matter? It wasn't even worth thinking about. Of course he wasn't the least bit angry about it. Of course not. Why should he be? The way things were now, she had every right to do as she damn well pleased. If she wanted to invite Haney Kenrick up here and jump into bed with that fat greasy pig, then all right. Let her do it with Haney every night in the week, if that's what she wanted. Let Haney give her gifts, give her money, give her all the jazzing he was willing to pay for.

59

Cassidy turned away from the bed and moved toward the closet. He told himself to hurry and collect his belongings and get the hell out.

He opened the closet door. It was empty. He stood there blinking. The closet should have contained three suits and some slacks and a few pairs of shoes. The shelf at the top should have displayed at least a dozen shirts and an equal number of shorts and some socks and handkerchiefs.

But none of it was there. Just an empty closet.

Then he saw the slip of paper hooked onto a clothes hanger. He snatched at the paper and stared at her handwriting. He read the message half aloud. "If you want your clothes, go drag the river."

Cassidy mashed the note in his fist. He raised his arm high and slammed the ball of paper to the floor. He aimed a kick at the closet door and as it banged shut some splinters flew from the broken wood.

He whirled about and saw the door of the other closet, the closet where she kept her clothes. He nodded grimly, crossed the room, telling himself what a fine time he would have, ripping every last dress to shreds with his bare hands.

He pulled the door open and the closet was empty. The emptiness of the closet was like a face grinning at him. And then he saw another slip of paper, also hooked to a hanger. He took it off and read it in a hissing whisper. It was only three words, the middle word her favorite verb.

The slip of paper drifted away from his hand. For some unaccountable reason the rage also drifted away and all he felt was a weird kind of sadness. Contained in it was a measure of self-pity. He was telling himself that some fools might think it funny. But there wasn't anything funny about a man losing every last goddamn stitch of clothes he owned.

He gazed at the floor and shook his head slowly. What a cheap trick. What a lousy, rotten, shameful thing to do. For Christ's sake, if she wanted to get back at him she could have tried something else, couldn't she? Or at least she could have left him a shirt to put on his back, just one shirt.

Then the rage came roaring back again and he jerked his

head sideways and saw the dresser. He was thinking in terms of her bottles of toilet water, jars of creams, her lingerie, anything. Anything that he could get his hands on.

The drawers of the dresser were empty. The emptiness of the final drawer was too much for him and he pulled it out all the way, pitched it across the room. It went flying through the doorway into the living room and crashed into a table.

Moved out, he said to himself. Threw all his clothes in the Delaware and then got all her things together and moved out. He told himself her best move right now was to be on a train going out of town, because so help him, if she was anywhere in the vicinity, and if he laid his hands on her—

The helpless rage almost choked him as he walked out of the flat and started downstairs. As he left the tenement and came out into the night air his fists itched with the need to hit something. He turned a corner and he was telling himself to get in touch with Shealy. He'd ask Shealy to open up the chandlery and sell him some clothes. He knew Shealy would be in Lundy's Place, because Shealy was always at Lundy's Place after working hours.

Cassidy started down Dock Street, going toward Lundy's. He knew he was in a hurry and couldn't understand why he wasn't speeding it up. He realized fully that he was walking slowly, almost with caution. And then the darkness of the street was acutely apparent to him. And the quiet of the street had a certain pressure, almost a weight that he could feel behind his back. The feeling grew and gradually it became the definite knowledge of approaching danger.

He had no idea what it was. Or why it was happening. But just as sure as he had two feet on the ground he knew they were moving in behind him and he was going to be jumped.

Just as he reached that conclusion he started to turn his head, to look behind him. In that moment they jumped him. He felt the blasting contact of something very hard coming down on his shoulder, knew it had missed his skull by inches. He ducked, pivoted, and saw the three of them.

They were three big men, hulking water-front roughnecks.

61

One of them was very tall and completely bald and had enormous hands. Another was built along the lines of a block of granite and had a mashed nose and twisted ears. The third man was very short, very wide, and carried a length of lead pipe. Cassidy didn't know any of them. All he knew was that there were three of them and someone had paid them cash to do a job on him.

The lead pipe came swishing again at his head and he weaved to one side. He wasn't thinking of the lead pipe. He was thinking of his clothes at the bottom of the Delaware, the rotten trick that had been played on him and the fact that only minutes ago he had been wishing he could bash his fists into something. He saw the lead pipe coming at him once more and instead of trying to get away from it he threw his arm out, grabbed at it, caught it, pulled it and took it away from the short, wide man. Cassidy brandished the heavy pipe in mid-air.

The two taller men came at him from either side but he paid no attention and walked in on the short, wide man and chopped with the lead pipe, catching the chunky target in the ribs. He let out a screech and doubled up and collapsed. The other men were in close and swinging at Cassidy and the big bald man caught him a crashing blow on the side of the head. Cassidy dropped the lead pipe as he fell back, and the full moon above his eyes became a pattern of many moons of different colors. He told himself it couldn't be that bad, he wasn't quite ready to go out. And somehow he managed to stay on his feet.

He grinned at the two men as they advanced. Then, as they came in quickly, he rushed at them and had his left hand shooting out like a piston, catching the bald man in the eye. And again. And trying to get rid of the bald man in a hurry, because the primary trouble was the other man, the man with a mashed nose and twisted ears. That was a professional. That had been in the ring, in far too many rings, as the wrecked face testified. But it could still move and know its way around. And it could still hit.

The bald man tried to duck under Cassidy's continued jabbing as Cassidy circled away from the plodding advance of the man with the mashed nose. Cassidy feinted with his right, jabbed the left again, then came in very close to blast with the right so that it hit solid and smashing on the turn of the jaw just under the ear. The bald man raised his arms slowly, spread his fingers, and fell, senseless.

In that same instant the man with the mashed nose threw a left hook that caught Cassidy under the heart and Cassidy went down. The man grinned at him and gently beckoned him to get up. Cassidy started to get up and the man reached down and grabbed him under the arms and helped him up, then knocked him down again with a right hook to the head.

The short, wide man had risen and taken hold of the lead pipe. With his other hand he held his burning broken ribs as he walked in and said, "now let me have him."

"Naw," the pug said, grinning. "This is mine."

"You're just playin' with him," the chunky man said.

"Playin'?" The pug reached down to lift Cassidy off the ground. "I wouldn't say that." He was holding Cassidy upright and not even looking at Cassidy. "I think I'm doin' a fair job."

But it was too casual. The pug was taking too much for granted. Cassidy swung a low, underhand right that was intentionally very low. The pug's mouth opened wide. A scream came out.

"Oh, no!" the pug screamed, walking away with his hands pressed against his body. "Oh, Jesus, no."

Then the pug sat down in the gutter and screamed and sobbed and said he was dying. The short, wide man took a tentative step toward Cassidy, saw Cassidy all set and ready for him, and decided it wasn't a good risk. The short, wide man dropped the lead pipe and started to walk away fast, and then ran.

In the gutter the pug had stopped screaming. The sobs were gradually subsiding. Cassidy came over to him and said, "Who paid you?"

"I can't talk. Hurts too much."

"Just tell me his name."

"Can't talk."

"Listen, John—"

"Aw, leave me alone," the man sobbed.

"You'll talk, John. You'll tell me his name or we'll see the police."

"Police?" The pug forgot to sob. "Aw, look, gimme a break."

"All right. Just give me his name."

The pug took his hands away from his groin. He inhaled deeply, his head flung back. He said, "Named Haney. Haney Kenrick."

Cassidy walked away. He walked fast along Dock Street, going toward Lundy's Place.

As he entered Lundy's, he saw Pauline and Spann and Shealy at their table in the far corner. He made his way to the table and saw them staring at his face. He wiped some blood away from his lip and sat down.

"Who jumped you?" Spann asked.

"Never mind," Cassidy said. He looked at Shealy. "Do me a favor. I need some clothes. You got anything my size in the store?"

Shealy stood up. "Should I bring it here?"

Cassidy nodded. "If I'm not around when you come back, leave it with Lundy. Bring some shirts, pants, a whole outfit. I'll pay you Friday."

Shealy put his hands behind his back and looked down at the table. "It'll save time if I just take it over to Doris."

"You stay away from Doris," Cassidy said. His gaze moved and included Pauline and Spann. "All of you, stay away from Doris."

"What goes on here?" Pauline asked.

"A reformation," Shealy murmured.

"Now, look," Cassidy said to Shealy. "I'm in a hurry and I don't want a discussion. You gonna get me some clothes or not?"

Shealy nodded. He smiled sadly at Cassidy and left the table and walked out of Lundy's Place.

Cassidy leaned his head toward Spann. "Tell me one thing. Just one thing. Where does Haney live?"

Spann started to open his mouth. But Pauline had her hand on Spann's arm and she said, "Don't tell him. Look at his eyes. He'll wind up in a lot of trouble."

Spann looked at Pauline. "Fade." he said.

"But look at his eyes—"

"I said fade." Spann made a very short and quick gesture with his forefinger.

Pauline rose from the table. She backed away across the room and bumped into another table. She sat down on the table top and stared across at Spann and Cassidy.

Spann was saying, "She's right. You look bad."

"Where does Haney live?"

"You look very bad, Jim. I can tell you're not thinking. You're in a mean, crazy frame of mind." Spann poured a drink and shoved it toward Cassidy.

Cassidy looked at the drink. He started to push it aside. Then very quickly, as though to get the process over with, he lifted the glass and shot the liquor down his throat. He lowered the glass and stared at it and said, "You gonna tell me?"

"If I'm sure you won't get yourself in a jam."

The drink was effective. Cassidy relaxed a little. He said, "All I want is to have a little talk with Haney."

Spann lit a cigarette. He inhaled very deeply and as he spoke the smoke came out in little clouds. "You want Haney fixed? You want it arranged so he leaves the neighborhood? Let me do it. I can make that adjustment."

"No, not that way. Not your way." And even as Cassidy said it, Spann was examining a long thin switchblade that had seemingly floated from somewhere into his hand.

"Nothing serious," Spann said. "Just carve him up a little. Just to give him the general idea."

"No," Cassidy said.

Spann gazed fondly at the blade of the knife. "It won't cost you a dime." He played the knife back and forth an inch or so above the table. "All I'll do is let him taste it, that's all. After that he won't amount to any kind of a problem. It'll guarantee he stays away from Mildred."

Cassidy scowled. "Who said I wanted that?"

"That's the issue, isn't it?"

"That's nowhere near the issue," Cassidy said. "The issue is me. Today he tried twice to put me in the hospital. Maybe even the morgue. All I aim to do is find out why."

Spann raised his eyebrows just a little. "Why? That's

easily understood. He knows you're blazing mad at him since this thing with Mildred. He figures you're out to get him. He figures he'll get you first."

Cassidy shook his head. "No, Spann. It ain't that way at all. He knows I'm finished with Mildred. For all I care he can have her all day and all night. Anyone can have her."

"You mean that?"

"You want me to print a sign? Sure I mean it."

"Yeah? Really?"

"For Christ's sake." Cassidy poured a drink and swallowed it. "Listen, Spann. I got myself a new woman—"

"Yeah," Spann said. "I heard all about it. Shealy told us." He smiled at Cassidy. "That's the way I like them. Thin. Real thin. Like a reed. Like that one over there." He floated his thumb backward, indicating Pauline. "I didn't know you liked them like that. How was she?"

Cassidy didn't answer. He looked at the bottle on the table. He estimated there were three drinks remaining in the bottle. He had the desire to take the three drinks in one long gulp.

"When they're real thin," Spann said, "it's like with a snake. They sort of coil themselves, don't they? Get their legs coiling, sort of. Thin like a snake, and coiling. That appeals to me. When they coil. The coiling." He leaned in a little toward Cassidy. "Did Doris do it that way?"

Cassidy continued to look at the bottle.

Spann said, "I'll tell you how Pauline does it. She reaches away back and grabs ahold of the bedpost. Then she—"

"Aw, choke on it, will you? I asked you where Haney lives."

"Oh, that," Spann said, his brain a screen on which a snake coiled and the face of the snake was the face of Pauline. "Oh, sure." He quickly mentioned Haney Kenrick's address and went on, "Then this is what she does. She—"

Cassidy was up and away from the table. He went striding across the room and out the front door.

The rooming house where Haney lived was a four-storied firetrap on Cherry Street. The landlady looked blankly at Cassidy as he stood in the doorway. She was a very old woman who smoked opium and Cassidy was only a meaningless blur in front of her eyes.

"Yes," she said, "Mr. Kenrick pays his rent."

"I didn't ask you that. What room is he in?"

"He pays his rent and he don't bother anybody. I know he pays his rent because I'm the landlady. He pays his rent and he better pay it or he goes out. All of them. I'll throw them all out."

Cassidy pushed his way past the landlady and went through the narrow hall leading into the parlor. Two old men sat in the parlor. One of them was reading a Greek newspaper and the other was sound asleep. Cassidy spoke. to the aged face behind the Greek newspaper. "What room is Mr. Kenrick in?"

The old man answered in Greek. But just then a girl in her early twenties came downstairs and smiled at Cassidy and said, "You looking for someone?"

"Haney Kenrick."

The girl stiffened. Her eyes were hostile. "You a friend of his?"

"Not exactly."

"Well," the girl said, "that sounds all right to me. Just so long as you ain't no friend of his. I hate him. I hate that man. You got a cigarette?"

Cassidy gave her a cigarette, lit it for her, and she said that Haney Kenrick's room was on the third floor, the rear room.

He climbed the stairs to the third floor and started down the hallway. It was quiet in the hallway and as he approached the door of the rear room he told himself to be careful. He wondered if it was possible to use the surprise method. With that method he would have a definite advantage. Without it, there was a real possibility that Haney would be prepared, and certainly it wasn't beyond Haney to depend on some kind of weapon.

Cassidy was at the door. He had his hand on the knob. He turned the knob, turned it carefully, very slowly. He heard the slight giving sound that meant the door wasn't locked. Then the knob turned all the way, the door opened, and he stepped into the room.

He stared at Haney Kenrick.

Haney was on the bed, face down, his legs dangling over the side, his feet touching the floor. His shoulders were shaking and he seemed to be in the midst of a laughing fit. Then he was rolling over and looking at Cassidy. His face was wet with tears and his lips quivered with despairing sobs.

"All right," Haney said. "So you're here. So you came to kill me. Go on, kill me."

Cassidy shut the door. He moved across the room and sat in a chair near the window.

"I don't care," Haney sobbed. "I don't care what happens."

Cassidy leaned back in the chair. He watched Haney's body quivering on the bed. He said, "You sound like a woman."

"Oh, God, God. I wish I was a woman."

"Why, Haney?"

"If I was a woman, it wouldn't bother me."

"Bother you? What bothers you?"

"Oh, God," Haney sobbed. "I don't care if I die. I want to die."

Cassidy put a cigarette in his mouth. He lit the cigarette and sat there smoking and listening to Haney's sobs. After a while he said mildly, "Whatever it is, I guess it's pretty bad."

"I can't stand it," Haney croaked.

"Well," Cassidy said, "whatever it is, I don't want you to take it out on me."

"I know, I know—"

"I want to make sure that you know. That's what I'm here for. This morning I get a brick heaved at my head. To-night I'm on Dock Street and I get jumped on. You paid them to make it complete."

Haney sat up on the bed. He took a handkerchief from his pocket, wiped his eyes, and blew his nose. "Believe me," he said. "I swear I got no grudge against you. It's just, I don't know, these past couple days have been hell, that's all." He rolled himself off the bed and made an effort to adjust his tie. His fingers were trembling and couldn't get

68

anywhere with the tie. His arms dropped limply and he sighed and lowered his head.

"Man," Cassidy said, "you're sure a sad case."

"I'll tell you something." Haney's voice was toneless with an emotional exhaustion. "For the past forty-eight hours I haven't had an ounce of food in my stomach. Every time I tried to eat, I choked on it."

"Try a cigarette," Cassidy said. He gave Haney a cigarette. It trembled violently in Haney's lips, and they used up three matches before they got it lit.

Haney dragged convulsively at the cigarette. He said, "I've had it coming. I asked for it and I got it. Oh, did I get it. Am I getting it." He tried to smile ruefully but instead his face twisted and became the grimace of a child getting ready to cry. He managed to hold onto himself and he said, "Can I talk to you, Jim? Can I tell you what she's doing to me?"

Cassidy nodded.

"But then again," Haney said, "maybe I better not. Maybe it's better if I keep my mouth shut."

"No," Cassidy said. "It's all right with me if you talk."

"You sure, Jim? After all, she's your wife. I had no business—"

"Listen, did you hear me? I said it's all right. I've tried to make it plain it's all over with me and Mildred. I told you that at Lundy's and I thought I got it across."

"Then, you're really finished with her?"

"Yes," Cassidy said loudly. "Yes, yes. Finished. Ended."

"Does she know that?"

"If she don't know it by now," Cassidy said, "I'll try throwing rocks at her."

Haney took the cigarette from his mouth, looked at it and made a wry face. He said, "I don't know. I can't understand it. That's what's driving me bughouse. It's the first time in my life I've ever had this grief. I've had all kinds of women and they've given me all kinds of trouble. But never anything like this. Nowhere near this."

Cassidy smiled dimly. He thought of the cigar stub in the ash tray and the crumpled sheets and the pillow on the floor. He said, "I can't see why you're crying the blues. You're getting it, ain't you?"

"Getting it?" Haney exclaimed. "Getting what?" He threw his arms out wide. "Getting red-hot pains in my stomach. Getting ruptured. I tell you, Jim, she's teasing me. She's teasing me."

"You mean you haven't had it yet?"

"Here's what I've had," Haney said, and he unbuttoned his shirt and displayed his bare shoulder. Three bright red fingernail scratches extended from the shoulder almost to the center of the chest.

"You better put something on that," Cassidy murmured. "Those scratches are deep."

"They don't hurt," Haney said. "Here's where it hurts. In here," and he tried to indicate his soul, his pride, or whatever it was that he valued within himself. "I tell you, Jim, she's tearing me apart. She's ruining me. Gets me worked up until I'm on fire. Then she pushes me away. And she laughs. That's what hurts most of all. When she looks at me and she laughs."

Cassidy pulled at his cigarette. He shrugged.

"Jim, tell me. What should I do?"

Cassidy shrugged again. "Stay away from her."

"I can't. I just can't."

"Well, that's up to you." Cassidy lifted himself from the chair and moved toward the door. "Only thing I can say is bashing my brains in won't solve your problem."

"Jim, I'm sorry about that. Believe me, I'm sorry."

"All right, we'll forget it." Cassidy turned and opened the door and walked out. As he moved down the hall toward the stairway he told himself it was settled. But as he started down the steps he felt uncomfortable. For some clouded reason he felt very uncomfortable. It was a dark, dragging feeling, as though he could see a shapeless, sinister force reaching out to touch him.

He assured himself the feeling would go away. In a little while he'd be with Doris and he'd be all right. Everything would be all right just as soon as he was with Doris.

His knuckles rapped lightly on the door. Doris opened it. He came into the room and took Doris in his arms. He lowered his head to kiss her and in that instant he smelled the

70

liquor on her breath. In the next instant he saw a large paper-wrapped package resting on the floor. His eyes narrowed and he began to breathe hard. He had taken his arms away from Doris. He was staring at the package.

She followed his eyes to the package. She said, "What's wrong, Jim? What's the matter?"

He pointed to the package. "Did Shealy bring that?"

Doris nodded. "He said you needed some clothes."

"I told Shealy not to come here." He moved toward the package and kicked it and it fell over on its side. He kicked it again, and then he faced Doris and glared at her.

She was shaking her head slowly. "What is it? What's bothering you?"

"I told that white-haired idiot to stay away from here."

"But why? I don't understand."

Cassidy didn't reply. He turned his head and looked at the kitchen doorway. He walked into the kitchen. On the table there was a half-empty bottle and a couple of glasses.

"Come in here," he called to Doris. "Take a look. Then you'll understand."

She entered the kitchen and saw him pointing at the bottle and the glasses. His pointed finger described an arc so that it aimed accusingly at her.

"It didn't take you long," he said.

She misinterpreted his meaning. Her eyes were wide with frantic denying as she said, "Oh, Jim, please. Don't get the wrong idea. All Shealy and I did was have a few drinks, that's all."

His eyes were blazing. "Whose idea was it?"

"To do what?"

"To drink, to drink. Who opened the bottle?"

"I did." Her eyes remained wide and she still had no idea why he was angry.

"You did," he said. "Just to be polite, is that it?" His arm swept out and he took hold of the bottle and showed it to her. "It wasn't here when I left this morning. Shealy brought it, didn't he?"

She nodded.

Cassidy set the bottle on the table. He walked out of the

71

kitchen and then he was at the front door, his hand turning the knob. He had the door open and he was about to rush out when he felt her fingers clutching at his sleeve.

"Let go!" he said.

"Jim, don't, please don't. You mustn't carry on like this. Shealy meant well. He brought me a bottle because he knows I need it."

"He doesn't know a goddamn thing," Cassidy snarled. "He thinks he knows. He thinks he's doing you a favor, holding you back and pulling you down. Dousing you with whisky. I'm going there now to warn him if he doesn't stay away from here—"

Doris continued to clutch at his sleeve. With a violence he didn't realize, he shoved her away, and she went staggering back and fell on the floor. Her lips quivered and she sat there on the floor rubbing her shoulder.

Cassidy bit hard at the side of his mouth. He saw she wasn't going to cry. He wished she would cry, or make any kind of sound. He wished she would curse him, throw something at him. The silence of the room was awful and seemed to multiply the self-hate he was feeling.

He said quietly, "I didn't mean to do that."

"I know." She smiled at him. "It's all right."

He went to her and lifted her from the floor. "I'm so sorry. How could I do a thing like that?"

She leaned her head against him. "I guess I deserved it."

"No, don't say that."

"But it's true. You told me not to drink."

"Only for your own sake."

"Yes, I know. I know." Then she started to cry.

She cried softly, almost without sound, but he heard the weeping and it was like a dull-edged blade slowly cutting its way through him. It seemed that he hung suspended in a void of futility, an area of endless discouragement. And the cutting pain was the knowledge that it was no use, it was just no use trying.

But then she was saying, "Jim, I'm going to try. With all my might."

"Promise me."

"Yes, I promise. I swear it." She lifted her face and he saw

72

the full meaning of her words in her eyes. "I swear I won't let you down."

He told himself to believe it. As he kissed her, he was believing it, he was cherishing the thought. The pain had faded and all he felt was the tender sweetness of her presence.

Chapter Seven

On the following morning Cassidy arrived at the depot and found a mechanic working on the bus. The mechanic was from a nearby auto-repair shop and was probably getting paid by the hour. He watched the mechanic for a while and then he told the mechanic to step aside.

It was carburetor trouble. The mechanic had complicated it and made it worse and now it presented a serious problem. Cassidy cursed and sweated for almost forty minutes. Just as he was making the final adjustments he saw the superintendent approaching with the mechanic and he braced himself for an argument.

The superintendent claimed that Cassidy had no right to interfere with a hired mechanic. Cassidy said the mechanic ought to learn his business before he allowed himself to be hired. The superintendent asked Cassidy if he had a chip on his shoulder.

Cassidy said he had no chip on his shoulder but it was his job to drive a bus and he couldn't drive it unless it was able to move. The mechanic muttered something and walked away. The superintendent shrugged and decided to let the matter fade. He turned to the waiting passengers and announced that the bus was ready.

It was going to be a full busload and Cassidy felt pleased because he and the bus were all set to take all these good people to Easton. The passengers were mostly elderly women and they were already in communion, the meaningless but nonetheless pleasant chattering communion of a lot of elderly women who were going to take a ride on a bus. They were all talking about what a nice morning it was and how they hoped they'd arrive in Easton in time to have lunch at this place or that place. And what a nice town Easton was. And what a relief to get away from Philadelphia for a change.

Then there were some elderly men who seemed to be going along on the ride for no special reason. A few of them had their grandchildren along, and the children were darting about like little beasts. One of the children was screaming for candy and when the demand was refused the child rebelled against getting on the bus. An elderly lady told the grandfather he ought to be ashamed of himself, it certainly wouldn't harm the little darling to have a bite of candy. The old man thanked her to mind her own business. They were blocking the doorway of the bus as they discussed the candy issue, and Cassidy told them to argue about it inside the bus.

The line of passengers moved slowly past Cassidy as he collected the tickets. Now the bus was getting filled and then it was all filled except for one seat. Cassidy stood there at the door and saw the final passenger coming through the turnstile. It was Haney Kenrick.

Haney wore a wide-brimmed dark-brown hat with a bright orange feather in the ribbon. He had on a double-breasted dark-brown suit that appeared to be almost new. His face gleamed pink and apparently he had spent the past half-hour in a barber shop. He smiled widely as he came up to Cassidy and presented his ticket.

Cassidy studied the smile. It was the exaggerated cheerfulness of a man who had spent the early morning hours with whisky. Haney seemed to have taken just enough of it to make himself feel happy.

Cassidy shook his head. "Nothing doing, Haney."

"But look, here's my ticket. I'm going to Easton."

"You don't want to go to Easton."

"Why, sure I do. I figure I'll work Easton today."

"Installment selling needs a car," Cassidy said. "Where's your car? Where's your merchandise?"

Haney was stopped for a moment. Then he said, ",Well, it's like this. Today I'll just case the town. I'll just look it over."

Cassidy saw the superintendent watching and starting to

74

move forward to hear what was going on. He knew he couldn't refuse Haney's ticket. He told himself to accept the situation and he said, "All right, get in."

He followed Haney into the bus and told himself to forget Haney. He concentrated on the idea that Haney was just another passenger. Settling himself into the driver's seat, he pushed the swinging lever that closed the door. Then he turned the switch and started the engine.

And then behind him there was some shoving and he glanced over his shoulder and saw Haney crowding an elderly lady. She was glaring at Haney and motioning with two pointed forefingers toward the rear of the bus, indicating a single vacant seat back there. Haney ignored her and moved clumsily, but sufficiently fast to take the seat directly behind the driver. The lady tossed her head with indignation as she started moving toward the rear of the bus.

Cassidy rolled the bus away from the depot, took it west on Arch to Broad Street, made the right-hand turn sending the bus into the heavy morning traffic on Broad. A red light stopped the bus and Cassidy saw a stream of smoke drifting past his face. He turned and saw the long, thick cigar in Haney's mouth.

"All right," Cassidy said. "Kill it."

"No smoking?"

Cassidy pointed to the printed sign above the windshield. He watched Haney pressing the lighted end of the cigar against the floor board. Then Haney brushed off the loose ash and gently placed the cigar in his breast pocket. Haney said, "Why no smoking?"

"It's a company rule," Cassidy said. "They got another rule against talking to the driver when the bus is in motion."

"But, now look, Jim, I got a few things on my mind—"

"Save it."

"It can't wait."

"It'll have to wait," Cassidy said. The light turned green and an Austin cut in front of the bus and he slammed on the brakes.

"Jim—"

"Ah, for Christ's sake."

"Jim, what ails you? I thought we settled things last night."

"So did I. Now you start the day with another discussion. But I'm working, Haney. I don't want to be bothered when I'm working."

"All I want to say is—"

"Shut up," Cassidy said. "Just sit there and shut up."

The bus went weaving in and out through the thick crawling parade of automobiles and trucks going north on Broad Street. It was difficult, delicate weaving that demanded Cassidy's full concentration and constant manipulating of the air brakes. The automobiles, especially the smaller ones, had a habit of darting out in front of the bus, passing on the right, stopping suddenly in front of the bus, continually worrying it as though it were a huge clumsy whale and they were killer sharks snapping at its sides. The ride going north up Broad Street was always the worst headache of the Easton run, and it had a nerve-racking resemblance to the job of trying to put jagged thread through a needle.

The automobiles were always making it miserable for him. There were times when he felt tempted to tag one of these pests and ruin a fender or two. The only nice feature about Broad Street in the early morning was the intersection at Roosevelt Boulevard where the heavy traffic came to an end.

Cassidy passed the boulevard, sent the bus past a succession of green lights, turned onto York Road and passed the city line. Now it was easy driving and he had the bus going at forty, cruising smoothly on the wide white-concrete highway aiming at Jenkintown. Through the roar of the engine he could hear the chattering of the elderly ladies, the giggling and shouting and occasional whining of the children.

A horn sounded behind him and he pulled slightly to the right. The horn sounded again and he glanced at the rearview mirror. As he reached out to tilt it he saw the automobile swerving out to pass him on the left. The automobile went past but he kept his eyes on the rearview mirror because it gave him a partial view of Haney and he saw a flask in Haney's hand.

He saw Haney taking the cap off the flask and lifting the flask and taking a long drink.

He turned his head slightly and said, "Put the flask away."

"No drinking allowed?"

He waited for Haney to put the flask away.

Haney said, "I don't see any printed sign."

"Put that damn flask away or I'll stop the bus."

"All right, Jim. No offense."

Haney lowered the flask into the inner breast pocket of his jacket.

The bus reached the crest of a hill and started down on a curving run that took it between bright green slopes with the sunlight splashing white on the road and yellow-green across the fields. The road going down was smooth and nicely banked and the bus made another turn and went riding onto level highway.

"Jim, we might as well talk it over."

"I said not now. Not here."

"It's important. I was up all last night thinking about it."

"What do you want, Haney? What the hell do you want?"

"I figure there's a way we can help each other."

"Listen," Cassidy said. "There's only one way you can help me. Get off my ear."

In the rear-view mirror Cassidy could see Haney's fat massaged pink face. Haney was perspiring and the edges of his shirt collar were wet. He had the dead cigar in his mouth and he was chewing on it.

"Well, it's up to you," Haney said. "You can settle it one way or another."

"Settle what?"

"The situation."

"There's no situation," Cassidy said. "There's no issue. At least not where I'm concerned."

"You're wrong. You got no idea how wrong you are. I tell you you're in a lot of trouble."

Cassidy told himself it was just talk, it meant nothing. But the feeling of apprehension hit him and then tugged at him, and he heard himself saying, "What kind?"

"The worst kind," Haney said. "When a woman starts to hate you. When she really has it in for you. I'm in the room with Mildred. She's sitting on the bed. She talks out loud like she's alone in the room talking to herself. She starts calling you a lot of names—"

"That ain't important," Cassidy cut in. And he grinned. "I've heard her call me every name in the book."

"You didn't hear it the way I heard it." Haney's tone was serious, almost solemn. "I tell you, Jim, she means to give you a bad time. A really bad time."

Cassidy went on grinning, to shove aside the apprehension. It allowed itself to be shoved, and he said lightly, "What has she got in mind?"

"I don't know. She didn't say what her plans were. But she did a lot of talking about you and that little skinny girl, that Doris."

Cassidy lost the grin. "Doris?" His hands tightened on the steering wheel. "One thing I know for sure. Mildred better think twice before she tries to hurt Doris."

"Mildred ain't the type to think twice. She's wild, she's vicious—"

"You don't have to tell me," Cassidy said. "I know what she is."

"You do? Maybe you don't. Maybe I know her better than you do." Haney took the cigar from his mouth, held it away from his face and looked along the length of it. "Mildred hits hard. She's a slugger. She can do a lot of damage."

"That's another thing I know," Cassidy said. "Tell me something new."

"She's out to smash you and make you crawl. That's what she wants. To see you crawl. She'll hammer you down until you're nothing. And I hate to think what she'll do to Doris."

Cassidy stared at the onrushing path of wide white concrete. "I don't think I get this. If you're playing poker, Haney, I'm not playing."

"It ain't poker. I'm showing you all my cards. You know I want Mildred. I'm dying a slow death because I can't have her. I'm thinking there's only one way I can win her over."

"That's what I don't get," Cassidy said. "You've set yourself on fire for this woman, you want her more than you want anything. But then you sit there and tell me I better go back to her."

"I didn't say that."

"You sure as hell let me know she wants me to come back."

"Crawling," Haney said. "I said that's all she wants. It ain't you. She don't want you. Only one thing she's itching to see. To see you flat on your belly, crawling back to her. So she can haul off and kick you in the face and send you crawling away. All she wants is the satisfaction."

"That's fine. You know when she'll get it? When the Atlantic Ocean dries up."

But then in the rearview mirror he saw Haney shaking his head.

And Haney said, "She'll get it, Jim. She's that kind. She'll find a way to get exactly what she wants."

"So what am I supposed to do?"

"Make it easy for yourself." Haney leaned forward. His whisper had a thick, oily quality. "For your own sake. And if you really care for this girl, this Doris, you'll be doing it for her sake."

"Say it, Haney. just say it."

"All right." The whisper became louder, and its oiliness was thicker. "I say you should go back to Mildred. But not like a man. Like a worm. Go on your knees, on your belly. Go crawling. And when she throws you out the door it'll be all over, she'll have had her satisfaction and that'll wind it up."

Just then a huge orange-and-white truck came rushing toward the bus. The bus was climbing a hill and the truck had negotiated a turn at the crest of the hill and swung too widely. The bus pulled over and the truck veered in toward the other side of the road. But it seemed there wouldn't be enough leeway. The bus appeared to shudder and cringe and then the truck swished past and it was all right.

"Close," Cassidy said.

"Jim?"

"I'm still here. I heard you."

"What'll it be?"

79

Cassidy's reply was a laugh. It was a hard, dry laugh and the taste of it was sour.

"Don't laugh, Jim. Please don't laugh." And now Haney had the flask in his hand and he was taking a drink. "You've got to do it, Jim. You can't do anything else. If you don't do it—"

"Jesus, man, cut it out, will you?"

Haney took another drink. "I claim it's the only way. It's the only thing that can be done." Then more liquor went down his throat. And then another drink and there was enough of it in him to make him completely subjective and he said, "I need Mildred so bad. And that's the only way I can get her. Right now she has only one thing on her mind. She wants that satisfaction. So do it, Jim. Do it, please do it. Go to her and let her throw you out. And then I know she'll look at me."

Cassidy laughed again.

Haney took another drink.

Haney said, "I've got some money in the bank."

"I told you to cut it out."

"I've got close to three thousand dollars."

"Now listen," Cassidy said. "I want you to shut up. And put that goddamned flask in your pocket."

"Three thousand dollars," Haney blubbered. He put his hand on Cassidy's shoulder. "Exact figure is twenty-seven hundred. That's my estate. My life savings."

"Take your hand off me."

Haney kept his hand on Cassidy's shoulder. He said, "I'll pay you, Jim. I'll pay you to do it."

Cassidy took hold of Haney's hand and pushed it away.

"Jim, did you hear what I said? I said I'll pay you."

"Drop it."

Haney took another drink. "You can use the money. It's good money."

"Forget it, will you? Drop it."

"Five hundred? How's five hundred?"

Cassidy rolled his underlip between his teeth and bit hard. The bus was climbing again and the top of the hill was white-hot concrete under the full blaze of the sun. The bus strained to reach the top of the hill.

"I'll make it six hundred," Haney said. "I'm willing to pay you six hundred dollars cold cash."

Cassidy opened his mouth, took a deep breath, then locked his lips tightly.

"Seven hundred," Haney said. He put the flask to his mouth and threw his head back. He took a long pull at the flask, and he had to drag it away from his face so he could talk again. He said hoarsely and loudly, "I know what you're doing. You think you got me at a disadvantage. All right, you bastard. You got me. I admit you got me. I'll give you a thousand dollars."

Cassidy twisted his head, started to say something, realized he didn't have time and he had to get his eyes back on the road. But as he faced the road again he could feel Haney's weight leaning on him, he could smell the full sloppy-sweet liquor breath of Haney. Now the bus had reached the top of the hill and it started the descent.

The road going down was curving, with the Delaware river curving in from the other side, so that the road and the river were a sort of forceps, the river bordered with another ribbon of water, the thin ribbon of the Delaware Canal. And far down there the canal was separated from the road by a barrier of big rocks. Past that there was another hill and it was very high. In order to negotiate the hill the bus had to gain a lot of speed going down. The bus went speeding down the hill. Cassidy could feel the trembling of the bus and he could hear the roaring of the engine.

As the bus went faster going down, Cassidy could hear the delighted cries of the children, and in the mirror he saw them hopping up and down in their seats. He saw the serious faces of the older passengers and the way they gripped the sides of the chairs. Then the mirror showed only one face and it was the face of Haney Kenrick, very close and very large in the mirror. Haney was leaning on him and he shouted at Haney to sit down.

Haney was too drunk to listen, too drunk to know what was happening. Then Haney tried to lean farther forward and in doing so he lost his balance. He reached out with both hands. His right hand sought the post at the side of the driver's seat. In his left hand he held the partially filled flask. He didn't know he was holding the flask, that he held it upside down so that the whisky was spilling onto Cassidy's head and face and shoulders. His right hand missed the post and as he swung over to reach it with his left hand he sent the flask crashing against Cassidy's head.

Cassidy was instantly unconscious and his chest came down on the steering wheel. One arm dangled and the other arm was hooked over the wheel, turning it. His foot pressed hard on the accelerator. The bus went screaming down the hill.

Then down toward the base of the hill the bus kept turning and it leaned over on two wheels, toppled there on the edge of the road as it continued to race its way down. It stayed on two wheels and then it was on no wheels and it rolled over, away from the road. It rolled over going down over the side of the hill. It rolled over and over. It kept rolling until it smashed against the big rocks near the Delaware Canal. The gasoline caught fire and exploded.

The wreckage of the burning bus was a blotch of orange and black on the sunlit rocks.

Chapter Eight

Cassidy had a feeling his head had been torn off and a new one made of cement had been set on his shoulders. He had to turn his head several times to see where he was. The last thing he remembered was being wedged in among some rocks, his lips pushed apart by something metallic, then seeing Haney Kenrick, the flask in Haney's hand, hearing Haney's quivering voice urging him to drink from the flask. He remembered the burning of the alcohol as it went down his throat, too much of it coming into his mouth and going down, so that finally he choked on it. And just before he went out again, he had looked full into the face of Haney.

Now a face came toward him. But it wasn't Haney's face. It was a narrow, aged face with thin lips and a sharp chin. Behind it there were other faces. Cassidy saw the uniforms

of State Highway Police. He centered on that for a moment
and then he came back to the narrow face of the seventy-
year-old doctor who leaned over him.

A voice said, "How is he?"

"He's all right," the doctor said.

"Any bones broken?"

"No, he's all right." Then the doctor spoke to Cassidy.
"Come on, get up."

One of the policemen said, "He looks hurt."

"He ain't hurt at all." The doctor closed his eyes hard, as
though trying to clear his vision. The eyes were red-
rimmed. It seemed the doctor had been crying. He looked
at Cassidy with something on the order of hate. "You know
you ain't hurt. Come on, get up."

Cassidy pulled himself from the rocks. He felt dizzy and
very much hung-over. He knew he had taken a lot of
whisky from Haney's flask. He wondered why Haney had
given him so much whisky, and wondered where Haney
was, and where the bus was. He sensed some pain at the
back of his head.

The sun hit him hard in the eyes and he blinked several
times. Then he saw the wreckage of the bus and he blinked
again. He saw the motorcycles and the official-looking cars
and the ambulances. A crowd of farmers and country people stood there along the side of the rocks and stared at
him. Everything was very quiet now and everyone was
staring at him.

Then he noticed Haney. And Haney was talking quietly
with several policemen. He started forward and a hand
came up against his chest. It was the hand of the doctor,
and the doctor was saying, "You stay where you are."

"What do you want with me?"

"You dog. You miserable drunken dog."

"Drunk?" Cassidy put a hand to his eyes. When he took
his hand away he saw the doctor taking a large syringe
from a leather bag.

A policeman who wore sergeant's chevrons came toward
the doctor and murmured, "No need to do it here."

"I'll do it here," the doctor said. "I'll make the test right
here."

The doctor took hold of Cassidy's arm, pushed the sleeve back and viciously inserted the needle of the syringe into Cassidy's forearm. Cassidy looked at the glass tube of the syringe and saw it filling up with his blood. He saw the satisfaction on the face of the doctor. The crowd had moved in, and there were women who wept softly. There were children who stared wide-eyed as though it were the first time they had seen anything like this.

Cassidy wanted a drink. He knew he needed a drink now more than he had ever needed one before. He saw the ambulances moving away. They moved slowly, as though there was no special reason for them to go fast. He saw the ambulances going away down the road. There were a lot of ambulances, and none of them went with sirens. Cassidy tried hard not to weep.

The doctor watched Cassidy's face working and said, "Go ahead and break down. You're gonna break down sooner or later, you might as well do it now."

Holding the syringe high, as though exhibiting it to the crowd, the doctor took a small glass tube from the leather bag, poured Cassidy's blood into the tube, corked the tube and handed it to the police sergeant.

"There it is," the doctor said. "There's your evidence."

The police sergeant put the tube in his jacket pocket. He came forward and took Cassidy's arm. "Let's go, bud."

Another policeman stepped in, and the police sergeant nodded, and the two of them walked Cassidy to a patrol car parked off the road near the rocks. The sergeant climbed in behind the wheel, beckoned Cassidy to sit beside him. The car started down the road. Cassidy opened his mouth to say something, knew he really had nothing to say, knew there was no point in saying anything.

They took Cassidy twelve miles down the road to a small brick building with a big sign in front that said it was a branch station of the State Highway Police. The sergeant went up to a desk and began chatting with a man who wore lieutenant's insignia. The other policeman took Cassidy into a small room and showed him a chair.

Cassidy sat down. He stared at the floor, rubbed his fingers through his hair. He saw the black leather boots of the policeman. The boots were very shiny. They appeared to be expensive boots. Probably the policeman liked expensive boots and preferred to pay for these out of his own pocket rather than accept the cheaper boots worn by other motorcycle policemen. Cassidy told himself to concentrate on the boots, to think about boots. He started to think about the wrecked bus and he begged himself to get back to the boots.

Finally he couldn't bear the silence and he raised his head and stared at the policeman and said, "What happened? Just tell me what happened."

The policeman was lighting a cigarette. He was young and tall and he had taken off his cap, displaying neatly combed straight black hair. He took a long puff from the cigarette. He took the cigarette away from his mouth and looked at the lighted tip. "You're in one hell of a mess."

"How do you know?" Cassidy felt the emphatic need to start defending himself.

"You were drunk. We got your blood in a tube to prove it. That tube'll show more whisky than blood."

The policeman moved toward a chair near a window and sat down and looked out the window.

Cassidy said, "I wasn't drunk when I was driving."

"Really?" The policeman continued to look out the window.

"I had that whisky after the crash."

"Really?"

"Before the crash I didn't have a drop." Cassidy got up from the chair and moved toward the policeman. "I have witnesses."

"You do?" The policeman turned slowly and looked at Cassidy. "What witnesses? That big fat guy in the brown suit?"

Cassidy nodded. "He's one."

"He isn't your witness," the policeman said. "He's ours. He said you were drinking all the way from Philly. He said you even got him loaded."

"Oh." Cassidy's voice was down to almost a whisper. "What about the others?"

"The others?" The policeman raised his eyebrows. "There aren't any others."

Cassidy lifted his hand slowly and pressed it hard against his chest.

The policeman watched him, studying him. Cassidy forgot the need to defend himself and he went on pressing his hand against his chest. He said, "All right, tell me."

"They're all dead."

Cassidy turned and walked back to the chair and sagged into it.

"All of them," the policeman said. "Every last one of them. Men, women and children. Twenty-six human beings."

Cassidy's head went down very low. He had his hands over his eyes.

"They couldn't get out of the bus," the policeman said. "They burned to death."

Cassidy had his eyes shut tightly but his eyelids were a sort of screen and on the screen he saw it happening. He saw the bus rolling down away from the road, rolling over and over going down to the rocks. He saw the door flinging open and himself and Haney Kenrick catapulted through the doorway onto soft grass, going away from the bus and toward the rocks. He must have sailed through the air, somersaulting across the grass to end up there in the rocks, and Haney must have landed nearby. The bus had landed on its side, all exits barred, the explosion coming fast, the fire gushing through the bus, and none of them could get out, not one of them could get out.

The policeman spoke softly. "You realize what you did? You murdered them."

"Can I lie down somewhere?"

"You'll stay where you are."

Cassidy reached into his jacket pocket and found his cigarettes. He put a cigarette in his mouth. Then he searched for his matches but he couldn't find them and he said, "Can I have a light?"

"Sure." The policeman came over and struck a match. He let the match burn brightly in front of Cassidy's eyes. "Look at it. Look at it burning."

Cassidy leaned the cigarette into the fire. He took smoke

into his lungs. The policeman stood there and allowed the match to go on burning before Cassidy's eyes.

"I wouldn't call it justice," the man said. "For them the fire ends everything. For you it lights your cigarette."

"Grow up."

"They died hard, mister."

"Shut your head." Cassidy gripped the edges of the chair. "If it was my fault I'd let you pound my face to a pulp and I wouldn't budge. But it wasn't my fault. I'm telling you it wasn't my fault."

"Don't tell me. Tell yourself. Keep telling it to yourself and maybe you'll wind up believing it."

The door opened and the sergeant stood there and beckoned. The policeman took Cassidy by the arm and they went out of the small room and into the main office where the lieutenant was talking to a group of policemen and men in plain clothes and Haney Kenrick. There was a strip of adhesive tape on the side of Haney's face and one of the sleeves of his suit was torn. Cassidy walked up to Haney and grabbed him by the throat with one hand and started to choke him. Haney let out a shriek, and the policemen closed in on Cassidy. They had to pry at his fingers to get him away from Haney's throat.

The lieutenant said, "Hold him. If he moves again, slug him." The lieutenant rose and circled the desk and came toward Cassidy. "Maybe I'll slug you myself."

Cassidy wasn't looking at the lieutenant. He had his eyes drilling into Haney's face. "Tell the truth, Haney."

The lieutenant pushed a finger against Cassidy's chest. "He told us the truth."

"How the hell do you know?"

"Now, don't get tough."

"I'll be just as tough as you are," Cassidy told the lieutenant. "You got your men holding onto the wrong party. You better tell them to let go of my arms."

The lieutenant hesitated for a moment, then told the policemen to let go of Cassidy.

Cassidy said, "What's the charge?"

The lieutenant leaned in close. "Driving a public vehicle while intoxicated. That's one. The other is manslaughter."

Cassidy pointed to Haney. "What did this man say?"

"Do I have to tell you what he said?"

"Yes. In detail."

"Man, you are tough, aren't you?" The lieutenant smiled tightly. "He said he was sitting right behind you. He said you had a bottle and you were drinking all the while you were driving. You offered him some and he had some, but you had most of it."

"That's a complete lie." Cassidy looked at Haney and Haney looked back at him with no particular expression. He showed his teeth to Haney. "Tell them about the flask."

Haney's frown was good acting. "What flask?"

Cassidy took a long breath. "You had a flask. I was out cold on the rocks and you came over and brought me to. You emptied half the flask down my throat."

The lieutenant turned and looked at Haney. There was a short quiet. Then Haney shrugged. "The guy's whoozy. I admit at times I do carry a flask. But not today."

Cassidy tightened the side of his mouth.

The lieutenant worked his eyes back and forth between Cassidy and Haney. "You men know each other?"

"Somewhat," Haney said.

"More than somewhat." Cassidy started toward Haney but the lieutenant blocked his path like a granite wall.

Cassidy's eyes were burning as he stared at Haney. Cassidy said, "It's a bright idea, but it won't work. Sooner or later you'll have to spill the truth."

Haney had no reply. The lieutenant frowned and showed Haney a puzzled face. "What's he talking about?"

"I guess," Haney began mildly, "he's only trying to protect himself. Wants you to think I pulled some kind of a frame." Haney made a relaxed, tolerant gesture. "Really can't blame the guy. If I was in his shoes I'd be just as frantic as he is. I'd try to sell you a wild bill of goods too."

The lieutenant nodded seriously. He came back to Cassidy and his mouth turned up at one corner. "It happens I got a lot of sales resistance." He turned away, looked at the other policemen, flicked a thumb toward Cassidy and said, "Lock him up."

Deep inside himself, Cassidy shivered hard. He knew he

couldn't allow them to lock him up because once they did it he would wind up in a courtroom and he realized what would happen in the courtroom. He realized he did not have the semblance of an adequate defense. It would be proven he was a drinker, he was a man with a shadowed past, and there had been nothing wholesome in the intervening years. The evidence would prove there was only one way for a bus to go out of control and roll off the side of a hill, as this bus had done, and the reason, without the trace of a doubt, was intoxication on the part of the driver. Testimony on the part of the sole and principal witness would blend with the evidence, and that was it, that was all of it.

He told himself he wasn't going to let them lock him up, he wasn't going to be put away for three years or five or seven or maybe more. His brain became ignited with animal rage and animal frenzy, and now, abruptly, he moved like an animal.

He moved against the shoulder of the nearest policeman, knocking the man against the side of the lieutenant's desk. Another policeman darted in and Cassidy stopped him with a fist going into the face, stopped a third policeman with a hard shove in the chest, then vaulted onto the lieutenant's desk. The lieutenant stared uncomprehendingly for an instant, grabbed at Cassidy's legs. Cassidy kicked the lieutenant's hand away, kicked hard at the window behind the desk, the broken glass flying like sprinkled water with Cassidy diving through, going out the window and hearing the yells behind him, hearing the thud as his shoulder hit the ground.

He was up and away from the ground, his feet churning him across gravel, then grass, his eyes taking in the parked motorcycles and patrol cars but not policemen because all the policemen were still inside the building. He was headed toward the highway, seeing the high grass on the other side of the highway, and beyond the grass a thick curtain of trees. As he raced toward the trees he could see the metallic sheen of the Delaware away out there and down and the purplish banks of the New Jersey side, a border between the water and the sky.

He ran very fast, going into the trees, twisting his path, his arms flailing at the interruption of twigs and branches. He didn't look behind him but he could hear them coming, he could hear the hoarse shouting of the lieutenant, and the lieutenant trying to curse and give orders at the same time. He begged himself to go faster, knowing he couldn't go any faster. He told himself they were going to get him, they would certainly get him, and he was an idiot to think he could get away. He kept telling himself they were going to get him and he ran faster through the thick woods and felt the downward sloping of the ground and saw the Delaware coming nearer.

Then the trees were behind him and the slope was getting soft and sandy, stones showing here and there, and rocks farther on down. Off to one side the slope ended abruptly, and he saw a ledge of jagged rock. He moved toward it, climbed onto it, went climbing up, hoping the ledge jutted out far enough so that he could try a dive into the Delaware. He came up over the side of the ledge, crawled out along the ledge and looked down and saw the water.

The water was very far down there. He told himself he didn't have much time to study the water. The ledge was somewhere around sixty feet above the water where it came lapping up against the side of the cliff. Directly down below it appeared to be fairly deep water in contrast to the areas on either side where the river flowed in toward sand instead of rock. He told himself it was sort of a lagoon down there and it might be all right. He had very little time and he had better quit thinking about it and jump.

He looked down and felt himself going feet first over the side of the ledge, going down very fast through the air, the water sliding up toward him, the air screaming in his ears. He hit the water, expected to meet blades of rock underneath the water, expected to die then and there. But all he could feel was the water, the deepness of it, the safety of the depth. He came up, looked out across the width of the Delaware, saw New Jersey about a mile away, wondered if he could make it before they put out after him with boats, or phoned New Jersey to pick him up when he hit the bank.

He knew he wouldn't be able to make it. He turned his head, saw he was only about thirty feet away from the cliff wall, saw openings in the cliff wall, a good many openings, some of them rather large. They looked like the beginnings of caves.

It was his only chance. He swam the thirty feet, reached up and grabbed rock, hauled himself onto the cliff wall, found another handhold, then a foothold, went on hauling himself up, ten feet, and then twenty, and finally reached one of the apertures. It wasn't wide enough. He peered up, and about ten feet above him, midway between the river and the top of the cliff, there was an opening that looked larger. He climbed toward it, going on a diagonal, and now hearing some shouts high above him. The shouts were faint but he could make out the words. They were up there on the slope on the left side of the cliff, telling each other the man had to be around here, he just had to be around here, he certainly wasn't in the river, they couldn't see him in the river. The voice of the lieutenant was somewhat hysterical, telling them to quit standing around, to start down the slope, to search every last damned inch of the slope.

Cassidy went on climbing. He gazed at the hole in the cliff wall, reached up, missed, and tried again and missed. He pushed his right leg against a fissure in the rock, kneed himself up, reached up again and this time he felt the edge of the hole. He tightened his hold on it, pulled himself up and up, his body leaning into the hole, crawling in.

He crawled in further. His breath came in gasps and suddenly he realized how much motion he had gone through, how tired he was. He flattened himself on the floor of the cave and closed his eyes. From somewhere far away he could hear the shouts of the lieutenant.

Later he found a chunk of large rock in the cave and he pushed it to the opening, so that it formed an obstruction in the opening, and from the outside, from the river, it would look as though the opening were quite small, certainly impossible for a man to get into. Huddling behind the rock he heard the voices coming from both sides of the cliff. That went on for perhaps an hour. He knew they would soon finish their search of the slopes and start examining the cliff wall. He wondered how intensively they would examine the cliff wall. Just then he heard the sound of motors in the river and he peered out from behind the rock.

They had their boats going up and down the river near the cliff. Policemen were standing in the boats, gazing up at the wall of the cliff. He saw they weren't using binoculars and he began to feel optimistic. There were a lot of boats in the water and they moved up and down and described circles, and after a while he realized the fleet looked just a little foolish. They were getting in each other's way. He knew he was really fooling them.

More boats sputtered over from the New Jersey side. The sun came down very hard and hot on the water and Cassidy saw the glittering impact of sunlight on the metal buttons of police uniforms, the shiny red faces of perspiring policemen standing up in their boats. Then there was a lot of shouting and considerable commotion and all the boats headed in a direction going away from the cliff wall. He leaned his head out past the rock and saw the boats going in toward the narrow strip of sand over on the right. He recognized the lieutenant jumping out of a boat, saw the lieutenant gesturing toward the slope, toward the trees up there, saw all the policemen scrambling up the slope. Some of them were pulling at their guns. They were going after someone who had been spotted on the slope or in the trees and obviously were quite certain this was their man. Boat after boat reached the sand and policemen were charging out and working their way up the slope. After some time the policemen came down and there was a conference on the sand. The conference appeared to be somewhat heated, and Cassidy heard the lieutenant stoutly defending himself against the loud statements of a big man who wore a straw hat and a tan suit. The big man seemed to be in charge of things and he would throw up both arms and then walk away and then come back and say something in a loud voice and then walk away again. This action went on and on and Cassidy saw shadows spreading out across the river and he knew the sun was going down.

Minutes later he saw the policemen going away in their

boats. Some of the boats were heading back to New Jersey. The other boats made a sullen, disconsolate parade down the river to whatever nearby dock they had come from. In the dusk the boats gradually became lost in shadow, and then it was all shadow, and Cassidy watched the river getting dark. He crawled back into the depths of the cave.

His clothes were still wet. It was not an uncomfortable wetness and he could feel warm, dry air coming into the cave, warming him, making him drowsy. He flattened himself on the floor of the cave, resting his face on his bent arm, lowering himself into sleep. He was almost fully asleep when a thought cut into the pleasant mist, and he lifted his head, glanced at his wrist watch. Despite his swim in the Delaware, the watch was still going. The luminous dial said eight-ten.

The wrist watch said twelve-twenty when Cassidy opened his eyes. He lifted his head, studied the watch, then turned and gazed out through the mouth of the cave. There was nothing out there but blackness. He crawled to the opening, looked down, saw the gleaming black water, looked up and saw the moon. He told himself it was time to go.

He wondered where he should go. It seemed logical that he should go as far away as possible. He should start thinking in terms of great distance. Automatically he developed the idea of hitting a port somewhere and getting himself on a boat and going to another country. For some reason it was not an attractive idea and he resented the state of things that forced him to ponder it. He did not want to leave the country. There was something here that he had started to build, and he wanted to continue building it; he wanted to stabilize and strengthen the foundation he had started with Doris. He had to get back to Doris. He had to let her know the truth of what had happened with the bus.

Leaning out of the cave opening, he saw moonlight coming against the cliff wall, glimmering on the sharp edges of rock. Off to one side, to the left, he could see a steplike arrangement of ledges that appeared to go all the way to the top. He maneuvered himself sideways, carefully feeling his way. He edged onto the nearest ledge, pulled himself onto the next ledge, then found the going comparatively easy.

The ladder of rock brought him to the summit of the cliff. From there he started across the slope, went into the trees, then through the trees to the highway.

His clothes were damp and the night breeze was chilly now. He stood at the edge of the highway and began to shiver. A car's headlights punctured the blackness far down the highway, and he ducked back into the trees, knowing he could not afford to be seen here in his bus-driver's uniform. He stood well back in the trees and watched the car go whizzing down the road. For some minutes he stood there and several cars went past, and a few trucks. Finally he realized he couldn't stay too long in this vicinity. He started moving along through the woods, parallel to the road, in the direction going back to Philadelphia. He knew the road well enough to estimate he was some thirty miles from Philadelphia.

He walked for an hour, rested, walked again, and another hour passed. Now most of the cars had vanished from the highway and it was dominated by the big trucks that traveled all night to and from Philadelphia. The big trucks moved swiftly down the road, their headlights lonely in the blackness. He watched one of the trucks lumbering past, his eyes following it hungrily as it went speeding away from his slow progress. Then it made a turn in the road, and there was a change in the sound of its motor. It seemed to be slowing down. He saw a glow coming from beyond the turn in the road, and acutely he remembered an all-night roadstand where the truck drivers stopped for a bite of food and some coffee.

Juke-box music flowed toward him along with the glow from the roadstand, and he crossed the road and went into the high grass on the other side. A minute later he was able to see the roadstand and the big trucks parked in the wide semicircle of gravel bordering the road. He worked himself through the high grass, studying the trucks, moving toward the trucks, finally selecting a trailer that belonged to a freight company located near the Philadelphia water front. The trailer was open in the back. He sneaked his way across the gravel and climbed into the rear of the trailer.

The truck was carrying tomatoes and lettuce and peppers. He knew it wouldn't make much of a meal but it might help to fill a definitely empty space in his belly. He sat there in the dark of the trailer and helped himself to the vegetables. Some minutes later he heard the driver climbing in behind the wheel. The truck moved out onto the highway.

In Philadelphia the truck cut away from Broad Street, went east to Fifth, all the way down Fifth to Arch, then east on Arch to Third. At Third the truck had to stop for a red light, and Cassidy climbed out, lowered himself to the ground and strolled across the street. He felt rested and somewhat confident. He thought of Doris and how near she was now, coming nearer, each moment bringing her nearer.

He walked quickly along Dock Street, then down the alley and saw the light in the window of her room. He came up and tapped gently against the window. The living room was empty and she was probably in the kitchen and he tapped again. There was no response.

The lack of response was something beyond mere silence. It was like a symbol, a message sent to him from an unknown region that did not exist in terms of time. It expressed something completely negative, a kind of dreary pessimism, telling him that no matter what moves he made, no matter what he tried to do, he just wouldn't get anywhere. The aching hollow pain of futility was almost tangible, as though he could feel the throb of internal bleeding. He knew that at this moment Doris was at Lundy's Place. She was having a date with her boy friend, the bottle.

Chapter Nine

He stood there at the window and shook his head slowly. There was no anger, no resentment. Now it was all sadness, and it was all the more dreary because he knew it was something that couldn't be repaired. She had let him down and she couldn't help it and it was just too bad. That was the only way to look at it. Well, anyway, he had tried. No matter what happened from here on in, he'd have that much to remember. He had tried hard. He had meant well. But the sum of it was failure and it was just too bad, it was a damn shame.

From beyond the tenement walls across the alley he heard a ship's horn sounding on the river. The sound was emphatic against the stillness of late night. It had a sort of beckoning quality, and he began to think in terms of the river, and the ships docked at the piers, and his chances of stowing away on a freighter. He started to move away from the window.

Then it occurred to him that he was very tired and he could certainly use a hot bath and a short nap before making a try at the piers. He turned, passed the window, and moved toward the door.

The door was open, as he knew it would be. In the moment that he entered, he wondered vaguely why he hadn't done this in the first place instead of tapping at the window. It might be that he had actually hoped there'd be no response to the tapping. That was a lot of damn foolishness, but at least it was consistent with every move he'd made since the exploded morning when a four-engined plane had crashed and burned.

It was weird, downright weird that right now he should be remembering that particular morning. He couldn't understand it. All at once he realized the blinding, shattering impact of a repeated catastrophe. On that day, the plane. And today, the bus. Scores of lives erased in the furnaces of a burning plane and a burning bus. He started to count the lives that had been lost and felt dizzy with the horror of it. The fact that neither crash had been his fault was not visible to him just now. All he saw was himself at the wheel, at the controls, himself responsible. He shut his eyes tightly and begged himself to quit thinking about it.

But there it was. The plane wrecked, the bus wrecked, and Cassidy at the controls. A good man to hire, this Cassidy. A very good man, if what they needed was a living hex, a wrong number, strictly a bad-luck operator.

Well, it was all over. It could never happen again. He'd

try to skip out tonight and if he made it onto a ship he'd keep on the move and spend the rest of his life in some faraway place where they couldn't find him. There were a lot of faraway places and it didn't matter which one he selected. As long as he got there. As long as he was able to hide. That was a pleasant thought, that was something to look forward to. A very pleasant future for Cassidy. For some odd, idiotic reason he wondered if they had such things as sleeping pills on some of these little islands very far away.

In the bathroom he shaved and then he filled the bathtub with hot water. He stepped into the tub and sat there and felt the steam going through him. As he came out of the bathroom and started to put on fresh clothes he was feeling a little better. But then again he thought of Doris, and Lundy's Place, and the back room reserved for customers who had to go on drinking after the two o'clock curfew. He thought of himself going away now, and leaving her there.

Forget it, he told himself. It's no use and just forget it. But he couldn't forget it. Well, then, what could he do? He certainly couldn't go to Lundy's Place. Sure as hell he'd be picked up. There was only one thing for him to do, and that was to forget it.

He lit a cigarette and rested himself flat on his back on the bed and tried hard to forget it. Something else crept into his mind but before it took shape he gave it a shove and forced it away. It stood on a little invisible shelf, looking down at him, and then he saw it was a blending of two faces. The face of Haney Kenrick, and Mildred's face. The faces were grinning at him. Haney's face went away and there was Mildred's face and she started to laugh at him. He could almost hear her voice saying, "I'm glad, I'm glad, it calls for a celebration and I'll buy drinks for the house. Give Doris a double shot. And you, Haney, where you going? Come on back, Haney, it's all right and you can sit with me. You're with me now, Haney. Sure, I mean it. Hear me laughing? That's because I feel so good. Because our friend the bus driver is getting it. The bastard is getting it, really getting smacked around. And you know what I'm doing? I'm eating it up. You did a swell job on him, Haney, you made it a

97

perfect job and you deserve a reward. Tonight I'll give you the reward. I'll really give it to you, Haney. The way only Mildred can give it. You'll get it like you never had it before."

Then it was in very close and smashing away at him and he felt the full blast of his rage. He was up from the bed, facing the door, his fists slightly raised, the knuckles very tight and hard. He made a move toward the door, knowing he was aiming himself at Lundy's Place, at the table where Mildred sat with Haney Kenrick. As he pictured himself lunging at the table he pulled his arms back and down and unclenched his fists. He turned away from the door and told himself to drop that sort of thinking. That was from yesterday, from all the rotten filthy yesterdays with a slut named Mildred. He'd better start thinking about tomorrow, and all the unpredictable tomorrows with a fugitive named Cassidy.

Jesus, he needed a drink. He looked around and couldn't see a bottle and wondered if there was one in the kitchen. As he started toward the kitchen he was grinning disdainfully. Grinning at himself. The noble reformer who had raised hell with Doris because she let Shealy bring her a bottle. And now he was going into the kitchen to see if he could find the bottle.

He was entering the kitchen when he heard the sound. The front door was opening. He turned and saw Shealy.

They looked at each other and the quiet was stiff, seeming to intensify the air.

Then Shealy closed the door behind him and leaned lightly against it. He folded his arms and he was looking Cassidy up and down.

"I knew you'd be here," Shealy said.

Cassidy's tone was icy. "What do you want?"

Shealy shrugged. "I'm your friend."

"I have no friends. I don't want any. You get out."

Shealy ignored that. "What you need now is some thinking. Some plans. You got any?"

Cassidy came into the front room and walked back and forth. Then he stopped and looked at the floor and said, "Nothing definite."

They were quiet again. But suddenly Cassidy frowned and stared at the white-haired man and said, "How come you know about it? Who told you?"

"Tonight's paper," Shealy said. "It's a front-page story."

Cassidy's stare went away from Shealy and aimed at nothing and he said, "Front page. Well, I guess that's where it should be. A bus is wrecked and twenty-six people burn to death. Yeah, I guess that does belong on the front page."

"Relax," Shealy said.

"Sure." He continued to stare at nothing. "I'm all relaxed. I'm doing fine. My passengers are a heap of dead ashes. And I'm there. I'm all relaxed and doing just fine."

"You better sit down," Shealy said. "You look like you're ready to drop."

Cassidy looked at him. "What else did the paper say?"

"They're searching for you. There's a lot of heat."

"Well, sure there is. But that ain't what I meant." He took a slow breath, opened his mouth again to say what he meant, then waved wearily as though it made no difference.

Shealy looked at him and into him and said, "I know what you meant. And the answer is no, there's not a chance they'll ever believe you. They believe what they heard from Haney Kenrick."

Cassidy's eyes widened. "How do you know Haney was lying?"

"I know Haney." The white-haired man went to the window, looked out at the street, up at the sky, then at the street again. He slowly pulled down the window shade and he said, "Let's hear your side of it."

Cassidy told him. It didn't take long to tell. It was simply a matter of explaining the accident of the bus and the strategy of Haney Kenrick.

At the end of it, Shealy was nodding slowly. "Yes," he said. "Yes, I knew it was something on that order." He ran his fingers through the soft gloss of his white hair. "What happens now?"

"I skip."

99

Shealy inclined his head. His eyes narrowed just a little. "I don't see you skipping."

Cassidy stiffened. "I came here to take a bath and rest up."

"Is that all?"

"Now look," Cassidy said. "Let's drop it."

"Jim—"

"I said we'll drop it." He walked across the room and lit a cigarette and took a few puffs. Just to say something he said, "I owe you some money for the clothes you brought. How much was it?"

"We'll forget that."

"No," Cassidy said. "How much?"

"Around forty."

Cassidy opened a closet door, lifted wrinkled trousers from a hanger, reached in and took out a roll of paper money. He counted off eight five-dollar bills and handed them to Shealy.

Shealy pocketed the money and looked at the roll in Cassidy's hand. "What you got there?"

Cassidy flipped the roll with his thumb. "Eighty-five."

"That isn't much."

"It'll be enough. The way I'll travel, I won't buy tickets."

"What about liquor?" Shealy asked.

"I won't be drinking."

"I think you will," Shealy said. "I think you'll be doing a lot of drinking. I estimate at least a quart a day. That's about average when they're on the run."

Cassidy turned his back to Shealy. He was facing the closet door and he said, "You white-haired bastard."

Shealy said, "I got some money in my room. A couple hundred."

"Stick it."

"If you wait here I'll get it."

"I said stick it." He grabbed the closet door and slammed it shut. "I don't want favors from anybody. I'm alone and that's the way I want it. Just to be alone."

"You're a sad case."

"Good. I like it when I'm down and out. I get a kick out of it."

100

"We all do," Shealy said. "All the bums, all the wrecks. We get to the point where we like that ride downgrade. To the bottom, where it's soft, where the mud is."

Cassidy had not turned. He continued to look at the closet door. "That's what you said the other day. I didn't believe you."

"Do you believe me now?"

The room was quiet except for the hissing sound as Cassidy breathed hard between his teeth. Deep inside himself he was sobbing. He turned very slowly and saw Shealy standing near the window, smiling at him. It was a knowing smile, and it was gentle and sad.

Cassidy's eyes went past Shealy, went through the window shade and the walls of tenements and the dark gray filth of the water front. "I don't know what I believe. There's a part of me says I shouldn't believe in anything."

"That's the sensible way," Shealy said. "Just wake up every morning and whatever happens, let it happen. Because no matter what you do, it'll happen anyway. So ride with it. Let it take you."

"Down," Cassidy murmured.

"Yes, down. That's why it's easy. No effort. No climbing, Just slide down and enjoy the trip."

"Sure," Cassidy said, and he worked his lips into a grin. "Why shouldn't I enjoy it?"

But the thought of it was not enjoyable. The thought of it was contrary to what he wanted to think. A moment of whizzing memory went shooting through his brain, and he saw a college campus, he saw an Army bomber, he saw La Guardia Airfield. And the flashed image, of himself in one of the finer restaurants in New York. He sat there with clean hands, clean shirt, his hair was clipped neatly. The girl across the table was sweet and slender, a Wellesley graduate, and she was telling him he was really very nice. She was looking at his immaculate hands—

He looked at Shealy. "No," he said. "No, I don't believe you."

Shealy winced. "Jim, don't say that. Listen to me—"

"Shut up. I'm not listening. Go look for another customer."

He moved past Shealy, aiming at the front door. Shealy was fast and went sliding in to block the door.

"Damn you," Cassidy said. "Get out of my way."

"I won't let you go there."

"I'm going there to talk to her. I'll bring her back here and sober her up. Then I'll take her with me."

"You fool. They'll grab you."

"That's the gamble. Now, get away from the door."

Shealy didn't move. "If you take Doris away from here, you'll be killing her."

Cassidy stepped back. "What the hell do you mean?"

"Didn't I tell you? I tried to make it clear. There's nothing you can give Doris. What you would do is take away the one thing that's keeping her alive. The whisky."

"That's a lie. That's the kind of talk I can't stand." He took a step toward Shealy.

And Shealy stood there, not moving. Shealy said, "All I can do is tell you. I can't fight you."

He waited for Shealy to move. He told himself he mustn't hit Shealy. His face was twisted as he snarled, "You lousy rumpot. You're a walking disease. I ought to bash your brains in."

Shealy sighed and bent his head slowly and said, "All right, Jim."

"You'll see it my way?"

Shealy nodded. His voice was toneless and very tired. "It's a pity I couldn't get the idea across. But I tried. I sure tried. All I can do is make the necessary arrangements."

"Like what?"

"I'll put you on a boat. Then I'll bring Doris."

Cassidy looked sideways at Shealy and said, "Is this the business? It better not be."

Shealy was opening the door. "Come on," he said. "There's a freighter at Pier Nine. Leaves at five in the morning. I know the captain."

They walked out and moved quickly down the alley toward Dock Street.

Chapter Ten

It was almost four now as they approached the piers. The night had reached the full pitch of darkness and the street lamps had been turned off and the only lights were the tiny lights here and there along the sides of the ships. As they came onto Pier Nine they could hear the dim sound of activity on the deck of the freighter. It was an orange-and-white ship, a converted Liberty. The paint was new and the ship was shining there in the darkness.

A pier watchman came toward them. Cassidy cursed under his breath. He had seen the watchman now and then in Lundy's Place and he was sure he would be recognized. He tensed himself, started to turn away. Shealy grabbed his wrist and said, "Easy, easy."

The watchman said, "What are you doing here?"

Cassidy had pulled up the collar of his jacket. He had his face averted. He heard Shealy saying, "We got business with Captain Adams."

"Yeah? What kind of business?"

"Are you blind? This is Shealy. From the Quaker City Chandlery."

"Oh," the watchman said. "Oh, sure. Go on up."

The watchman turned away and went back to his little shed and the sandwich he'd been eating in there.

They climbed the ladder going up to the deck of the ship and climbed over the rail. Shealy told him to wait there at the rail. He leaned back against the rail and watched Shealy walking along the deck, then rounding the deck. He lit a cigarette and told himself he wasn't nervous. He stood there at the rail, smoking nervously.

A few seamen walked past him and ignored him. He started to like the feeling of being here on the ship. It was the best place for him to be. Soon it would be leaving the port and going away and he would be on it. With Doris. On the ship and going away with Doris. That was what he wanted and he was deeply certain that Doris wanted it and soon it would be happening, just like that.

Then Shealy reappeared, accompanied by a tall, middle-aged man who wore a captain's cap and had a meerschaum pipe in his mouth. He was looking Cassidy up and down and then he was looking at Shealy and shaking his head.

Cassidy moved away from the rail and went toward them and he heard Shealy saying, "I'm telling you he's all right. He's a friend of mine."

"I said no." The captain gazed calmly across the deck and out upon the river. "I'm sorry, but that's the way it is." He turned his head to look at Cassidy. "I'd like to help you, mister, but I just can't afford the risk."

"What risk?" Cassidy murmured. He scowled at Shealy. He knew that Shealy had put all the cards on the table.

Shealy said, "Jim, this is Captain Adams. I've known him for years and he's a man to be trusted. I've told him the truth."

Adams smiled thinly at Shealy. "You did that because you know I can always smell a lie."

"The captain's a brilliant man" Shealy told Cassidy."He's highly educated and the thing he understands most is people."

Cassidy felt the captain's eyes going into him, examining him. It was as though he was being lifted with tweezers and placed under a lens, and he didn't like it. He gazed sullenly at the captain and said, "I don't have much time. If we can't do business I'll try another boat."

"I wouldn't advise that," Adams said. "What I think you should do is—"

"Save it." Cassidy turned away and he was moving toward the ramp. He started to climb over onto the ladder and felt a hand on his shoulder. He thought it was Shealy and he jerked his shoulder away and said, "If you're coming, come on. I don't need this action."

But then as he looked, he saw it was the captain. He saw the smile on the face of the captain. It was an intelligent smile and it was sort of objective.

"You're an interesting case," Adams said. "I'm thinking maybe I'll take the risk."

Cassidy was halfway over the rail. He saw Shealy hurrying forward. Shealy said, "It's a good risk, Adams. You have my word on that."

"I don't want your word," the captain said. "I just want a few minutes alone with this man."

He backed away from the rail and beckoned to Cassidy. He kept moving backward across the deck and Cassidy came toward him. Then they were standing facing each other near a hatchway.

Adams said, "You can't blame me for being careful."

Cassidy said nothing.

"After all," Adams said, "I'm the captain of this ship. I'm held responsible."

Cassidy put his hands behind his back. He looked down at the dark, shining deck.

"I lost a boat once," Adams murmured. "In Chesapeake Bay. It was during a fog and we ran into a steamer. They said I ignored the signals."

"Did you?"

"No. There weren't any signals. But they fixed that at the investigation. The steamer belonged to a big company. I heard my own men talking against me. I knew they'd been paid."

For a moment it seemed to Cassidy that he was alone. He said aloud to himself, "No way to prove it. Not a damn thing you can do."

"I did something," Adams said. "I ran away. I ran very far away and then gradually I made a comeback." He moved in closer to Cassidy. "Did you wreck that bus today? Was it your fault?"

"No."

"All right, that's settled. I believe you. But there's something else that bothers me. The woman."

"I won't go without her."

"Shealy said you have a wife."

Cassidy turned away from the captain and walked across the deck and came up to Shealy. He said, "You fixed it your way, didn't you? In other words, he'll take me but he won't take Doris."

"You've got a chance here," Shealy said. "Don't lose it."

105

"The hell with that." Cassidy pushed Shealy aside. Again he was at the rail.

And again the hand was on his shoulder. He knew it was Adams. He heard Adams saying, "You're a damn fool. And I'm a damn fool."

"What is this?" Shealy said.

"It's a mistake," the captain told Shealy. "I know it's a mistake and I think this man Cassidy knows it. But we're doing it anyway." His hand described a slow, weary gesture away from the rail. "Go bring the woman."

Shealy shrugged and put his hands on the rail and started to climb over. But then Cassidy caught his wrists and held him there and said, "I want you to promise."

"You see me going, don't you?"

"That ain't enough. I want to be sure about this."

"I'll do the best I can."

"Now look, Shealy, I'm in no position to make demands. You've gone to bat for me tonight and I want to thank you for it. But a favor ain't a favor unless it goes all the way. If you don't bring Doris it'll ruin everything for me. Promise me you'll bring her."

"Jim, I can't promise that. I can't make decisions for Doris."

"It won't need a decision. You know as well as I what condition she's in. This time of night she's sitting there in Lundy's dead drunk. Just take her home and pack her clothes in a bag. Then bring her here."

"Drunk?"

"Drunk or sober, I want her here."

Shealy tightened his mouth to a thin line. He swallowed hard and said, "All right, Jim. I promise."

Cassidy stood at the rail and watched Shealy going down the ladder.

It was a few minutes later and Adams was opening a door for him and saying, "Here's your cabin."

The room was small but he saw it had a double bed and there was a rug on the floor and a chair near the porthole. There was a dresser and a washstand. He told himself Doris would be comfortable here.

Adams was lighting the meerschaum. He held the lighted match away from the bowl, studied the glowing tobacco, took a speculative puff and blew out the match. He said, "When the lady comes aboard, shall I send her here?"

Cassidy smiled. "Where else?"

The captain wasn't smiling. "I didn't want to take anything for granted. If you wanted separate cabins—"

"She stays with me," Cassidy said. "She's my woman."

Adams shrugged. He turned to face the door. He moved toward the door, started to open it, then changed his mind and came back to Cassidy. His eyes were solemn.

"It's a long cruise."

"Where to?"

"South Africa."

Cassidy widened his smile. "That's fine. I like that." Then abruptly he remembered something and he said, "What'll it cost?"

Adams waved it aside. "It's all arranged."

"Shealy?"

The captain nodded. "You can pay him back when you have it. He'll be in no hurry."

Cassidy sat on the bed. "When I have it," he said aloud to himself. He looked up at the captain. His smile was slightly twisted. "How are things in South Africa?"

"They get along." The captain knew it was going to be a conversation and he came around past Cassidy and took the chair near the porthole. He glanced at a pocket watch and murmured, "Forty minutes. Plenty of time." Then his eyes were calm and old and wise, looking at Cassidy, and he said, "No matter where it is, South Africa or anyplace else, it's never easy when you have a woman on your hands."

Cassidy said nothing.

"If you were going alone," the captain said, "you wouldn't be worrying about the finances."

Cassidy looked at the captain and decided to say nothing.

"She's a healthy girl?" the captain asked. "You sure she can stand the trip?"

Cassidy told himself to let the captain keep talking.

Adams took a long drag at the meerschaum. "It's a rough

trip. This is no pleasure boat. My crew does a job, but you know how it is. They get bored now and then. Restless. Sometimes they get mean. And when there's a woman aboard—"

"I'll worry about that."

"Mainly it's my worry," Adams said. "I'm responsible for my passengers."

Cassidy stared at the floor. "Just run the boat, Adams. Get the boat across the ocean."

"Yes," Adams said. "That's the main thing. To take the boat across and bring it into port. But then there's all the other things. That's the way it is with the captain of the ship. The captain is responsible for the crew, for the passengers. If anything happens—"

"It won't."

Adams puffed slowly at the meerschaum. "I wish that was a guarantee."

"I'll make it a guarantee," Cassidy said. He stood up. He was getting angry and worried and unhappy. He told himself it was all right to be angry, but he had better get away from the worry and the unhappiness. That wasn't the way to start this trip. This trip was very important and it had great meaning and he mustn't think of it in terms of hazard.

Captain Adams was saying, "After all, when there's a woman aboard—"

"That's enough."

"I'm only saying—"

"You're saying too much." He glared at the captain. "You made a deal, didn't you? You trying to crawl out of it?"

Adams sat there comfortably. his ankles crossed, his shoulders relaxed against the cabin wall. "I made a deal and you can hold me to it. That is, of course, unless you change your mind."

Cassidy breathed hard. "You want me to change my mind? Why do you want me to do that?" He threw his arms out in a confused, somewhat frantic gesture. "Christ Almighty, man, you don't even know me. What's all the brotherly interest?"

"Fatherly interest."

"Ah, screw that." He turned away. He was breathing very

hard and a lot of thoughts were going through his mind and he tried to snatch at them to see what they were. But they were running too fast.

He heard Adams saying, "I'm trying to steer you right."

"It ain't getting across. I don't even hear you."

"You hear me and you know I'm making good sense. It's getting on your nerves because you have no way to answer me. You have no argument. It's just like Shealy said. Like he told me. He said this girl Doris is a drinker, a far-gone alcoholic, really in bad shape. He said—"

"The hell with what he said."

"Can't we talk about it?"

"No." Cassidy made a gesture toward the door. "It's my problem."

Adams stood up and moved toward the door. "Yes," he said, and he had hold of the doorhandle. "I guess you're right about that." He was turning the handle and opening the door. "It's your problem. And I can tell you it's a damn shame, it's a real heartbreaker. But if you want it that much, you'll sure have it."

Cassidy turned to say something, but Adams had walked out and the door was closed. He stood there looking at the door. It was an ordinary door made of wood but he was telling himself it was the door of a cabin on a ship going to South Africa. That made it a special kind of door. It was a very important door because soon it would open again and Doris would come walking in and then they would be here together in the cabin of this ship going out across the Atlantic Ocean, going southeast down across the Atlantic, going all the way down there down south to South Africa. With himself. With Doris. Going away together.

That was true. That would happen. And it was bound to happen, it was right and Shealy was wrong, the captain was wrong. They were wrong because they were weak. Just a pair of weak, washed-out old men who had long ago lost the vigor and the spine and the spark.

But he, Cassidy, he hadn't lost it. He still had it, packed solid and wedged in tightly and letting him know it was there. It was there in his mind and in his heart and he told himself he hadn't lost it, he would never lose it. It was the marvelous substance and fire and surging and as long as it was there, as long as it revolved and throbbed, there was chance, there was hope.

He moved across the cabin to stand at the porthole, and he looked out upon the dark water. The river pulled gently at his eyes, to show him the wider stretch of water beyond the river. And he knew soon it would be the ocean, he would be here with Doris in the cabin, looking out together through the porthole and seeing the ocean.

And crossing the ocean. With his woman, Doris. Going to South Africa. Eight or nine days on this ship on the ocean and then South Africa. probably Capetown, and he'd go out and find some kind of work, maybe on the docks there. He wouldn't have trouble finding work on the docks. They'd take one look at the bulk of him, his muscles, and he'd have a job. It wouldn't be much but it would pay the rent and bring in the food and then later he'd look for a better job. After all, South Africa was a big place and people traveled from city to city. They had busses—

He was shaking his head, telling himself he mustn't think of it. But there it was, he saw it happening, the bus rolling down off the road and then on two wheels and then on no wheels and crashing against the rocks and burning there. On the screen of his mind the flames were bright green and gradually there was silver in the green and it was the silver color of something that wasn't a bus. It was a fuselage. It was part of the big four-engined plane that had crashed at the far end of La Guardia Field, near the small bay, burning there in the swampland.

And yet, even as the searing and scorching and brightness of the flame were causing him to groan without sound, he told himself to get past it, to climb over it, to hurry and get away from it and think about South Africa.

Then again he was thinking about Doris and himself in South Africa. Now he was able to think about the fact that they had busses there and eventually he would have a good job driving a bus. But wait, hold it, be calm and very steady and just consider for a moment that in South Africa there were airfields, there were airlines—

Of course.

His hand slowly formed to a fist, and very slowly, as if in slow motion, he hit it against his palm.

Of course. Of course. It was possible, sure it was possible. And as he turned away from the porthole, his eyes were closed and he was seeing a big plane down there in the skies over South Africa. He was seeing the passengers in the plane, and the prim neat stewardess who spoke with a British accent. Of course they all spoke with a British accent and they were all polite and had that very nice quality of being able to mind their own business. Anyway, he was sure they would mind their own business to the extent of not asking too many questions. And if it went along that way, if there was just a small lucky break here and there, the pilot of that big plane would be Cassidy.

It had to be Cassidy. It was going to be Cassidy. The captain at the wheel, the man in charge, Captain J. Cassidy. And his hair would be neatly clipped, he would be shaved and showered and his hands would be smelling of soap, his fingernails spotless. The big plane would land and there would be the heavy and solid and wonderful sound of the big rubber wheels rolling firmly across the field. It would be there, the big plane arriving on time, and the passengers would come out down the ramp as Captain J. Cassidy made the final notations on his flight report.

And then, as he walked toward the terminal building, he would see Doris. She would be waving to him. He would see the radiance and the sweetness and it would become more wonderful with each step he took toward her. They were having dinner out tonight, a very special dinner to celebrate his first year with the South African airline.

They were in the fine restaurant in Capetown and the waiter handed them the menus. He turned the menu so that he was looking at the wine list. Then he looked at Doris and inquired if she would like to have a cocktail. She smiled and said she wouldn't mind having some dry sherry. He told the waiter to bring two dry sherries. He heard Doris telling him he was very nice company, he was really a very fine person. They sat there at the table and it was a wonderful dinner. It was lobster, and while cracking a claw he casually asked Doris if she would like some white wine with the lobster and she said not especially, but later on after the coffee it might be nice to have some muscatel.

Of course. That was the way it would be. That would be the extent of her drinking when they were together in South Africa. A dry sherry now and then. A small glass of muscatel. And with him it would be the same. There would be no need for the other kind of drinking. In South Africa it would be a life of quiet joy, the placid pleasures that had meaning because all the time it would be with Doris, it would be living with Doris and everything was going to be good and glowing. It was going to be proper.

Of course. And then he looked at the door of the cabin. And he smiled eagerly, because now he heard the footsteps coming down the corridor. The footsteps were feminine, and he stood near the door so that he would be there to embrace Doris the instant she entered the cabin.

The door opened and he stepped forward and then stepped back and he was rigid. He was looking at Mildred.

Chapter Eleven

He told himself it wasn't Mildred. It couldn't be Mildred. He backed across the cabin until his shoulders hit the thick metal rim of the porthole, and he saw Mildred slowly closing the door behind her. Then he watched the way she adjusted her hands to the full roundness of her tightly skirted hips and bounced lightly, brazenly on one leg as she looked him up and down.

He was trying to pull away from the shock and dismay of the long, shattering moment. He blinked several times and opened his mouth and closed it and then just stood there looking at Mildred.

She was glancing around the ship's cabin. There was a small mariner's ornament dangling on the wall, a brass anchor, and she walked over to it and flipped it a few times and said quietly, "Just where do you think you're going?"

She had her back to Cassidy. He saw the jet-black hair

112

shimmering thickly down along her shoulders. He said, "I'm going for a boat ride."

Mildred turned to face him. She took a deep breath that swelled her huge breasts until it seemed they'd come plopping out through the fabric of her blouse.

She said, "You think so?"

"I know so."

"But you're wrong," Mildred said. "It ain't like that. It ain't like that at all."

He glowered. "Ain't like what?"

"Ain't that easy." Then she turned and looked at the neat stretch of spread across the double bed. She reached down and patted it, as though testing the mattress.

Cassidy said, "How'd you know where I was?"

She continued to test the mattress. "Shealy."

He moved toward her and said, "You re a liar, You've had me spotted."

"Is that what you think?" She was planting herself comfortably on the bed, sitting there and leaning back on her elbows. "Go ahead and think it."

Cassidy wanted to walk back and forth, but the cabin was too small. Aloud to himself, he said, "Where's Shealy?"

Mildred had taken a pack of cigarettes from her skirt pocket. As she lit a cigarette, she said, "Your friend Shealy is at Lundy's place."

"What's he doing there?"

"What he always does. He's drinking."

Cassidy went to her and threw a grip on the fleshy part of Mildred's arm. "I said you're a liar." His fingers tightened on her arm. "You'll tell me the truth—"

Her smile was deadly-dangerous and she said, "Let go of my arm or you get this lit cigarette in your eye."

He released her arm. He moved over to the far side of the cabin and watched her as she continued to enjoy her cigarette. There was a thick, cut-glass ash tray on a table near the bed, and she reached over and placed the ash tray on the bed beside her.

"I'll finish this cigarette," she said. "Then we'll go."

"We'll do what?"

"I said we'll go."

113

His smile was an open sneer. "Go where?"

"You'll find out."

The sneer became a laugh. "I don't need to find out. I already know."

"You think you know. That's your big trouble."

Suddenly he was confused and there was the feeling of being helpless and he couldn't understand it. He scowled at her and said, "I want to know what you're doing here. What's your game?"

"No game," she said, and she shrugged. "It's just the way things are lined up. You belong to me, that's all."

"Listen," he said, "we had that out and it's all over. Now what you better do is forget it."

"You heard what I said. I said you belong to me."

Suddenly he was leaping away from the helplessness and he felt the rage coming and sizzling and he said, "You better get out of here before you get hurt."

She took a long drag at the cigarette. As the smoke came from her lips, she said, "If I go, you go with me."

He checked the rage and tried patience and said, "I'll wise you up to a couple of facts. In the first place I don't want to go with you. In the second place, I'm in no position to go anywhere except on this boat. Maybe you haven't heard about what happened today—"

"Yes, I heard. I know all about it. That's why I'm here." She had her eyes on the thick glass ash tray as she tipped ashes into it. "It's a tight jam but I'm sure I can get you out of it. If you listen to me, if you do as I say—"

"If I listen to you I'm a damn fool. If I do as you say I'll deserve exactly what I'll get. The business."

She mixed a frown with a grin. "You don't really mean that."

"The hell I don't."

"Well, I'll be—" She stood up. "You know what I think? I think you're doped up, or else you're crazy, or something. What's wrong with you?"

"Not a thing," Cassidy said. "It's just that I got my eyes wide open. I know what you want. You want to see me crawl. You'll do anything just to see me crawl."

She put a hand on her hip and put her other hand on top

of her head. She ran her fingers through the thick black hair. She just stood there and looked at him and didn't say anything.

"Sure," he said. "You know I've hit it right on the button. You don't want me, you never did want me. You wanted your kicks, that was all. And you liked it most when I was boiling mad. Or sometimes when I'd come home so tired I could hardly move, and you had your fun getting me worked up. Pushing those big balloons in my face. You sure had yourself a fine time—"

"And what about you? I didn't hear you complaining."

"Do you hear me now?" He advanced upon her. "You don't bother me any more. Can you understand that? You can jiggle and jiggle all you want and it don't do a thing to me. All I see is a fat slob doing a shimmy."

She inclined her head thoughtfully. "Fat slob? You call me fat? The way I'm distributed?"

He started to turn away and she grabbed him and swung him around.

She said, "You don't call me a fat slob. You'll take it back."

It was plain that she didn't want him to take it back, she wanted a battle, and he told himself if it came to a battle it might end disastrously for him. The exact nature of the disaster was obscure at this moment, but he realized he couldn't afford to have another battle with Mildred. He looked at her and he realized something else. She certainly wasn't a fat slob. She was all the other names he had ever called her, but she wasn't a fat slob.

"All right," he said. "I take it back."

He said it quietly, almost mildly. He saw Mildred biting her lip with disappointment and consternation.

"You see the way it is?" he said, and his tone remained low and relaxed. "The switch is busted. There's no ignition. You can't turn me on and off any more."

"Can't I?" She had her head lowered slightly so that her eyes blazed up at him through the long thick black lashes.

"No," he said. "You can't"

"And you're glad?"

"Sure. It feels a lot better. Like when they take the chains off."

115

"I don't believe you," she said, "I don't think of it that way." She bit her lip very hard She turned her face to the side and frowned deeply. As though he wasn't in the room, as though she wasn't saying it aloud, she said, "You're a case, Cassidy. You're a damned tough case to figure."

"Maybe I am." He turned his back to her and he was standing at the porthole and looking out. "I can't help that. That's me."

"All right," Mildred said. "That's you. And this is me. And what happens now?"

He saw some vague streaks of gray in the black sky and he knew it was getting on toward five o'clock. He said, "You can do me a final favor."

"Like what?"

He told himself to turn and face her. But somehow he couldn't take his eyes away from the river and the sky.

He said, "Get off this boat."

"Is that all?"

He detected something odd, almost sinister, in her voice and he frowned through the porthole at the dark river and muttered, "That's all I can ask."

"You can ask for more. Go on, give it a try. Maybe I'll come through."

"Listen, Mildred—"

"Don't build up to it," she told him. "Just make the request."

He took a very deep breath. He held it. He said, "Bring Doris."

As he said it he realized he had been lured into making a serious error. Beyond everything else was the blunt knowledge that he was dealing with a ferocious female and instinctively he started to turn and threw up his arm toward his head to protect himself. As he did that, he saw the flashing arc of the thick glass ash tray. She held it tightly and banged it against his arm and as he dropped his arm she hauled off again with the ash tray. The thick glass came crashing down upon his skull. He saw some fiery green triangles and circles of fiery yellow. He saw some wavy ribbons of very bright orange, and he felt the heat of the color. After that it was all black.

Chapter Twelve

There was considerable rocking and he told himself the ship must be hitting rough water. He sensed that the ship was going down along the trough of a high wave, and then there was a jarring feeling and that was probably another high wave crashing against the ship, taking it up again. He decided it was a really bad storm and the ocean was plenty mean and if it got much worse the ship would capsize and sink. It might be a good idea for him to go up on deck and see what was happening. Maybe he ought to wake Doris and tell her the ship was in trouble. He called her name but couldn't hear his own voice, only the roar of the storm that was smashing the ship.

Then it was as though there was no storm, the storm had passed and the ship had sunk. Somehow he had been rescued and they were taking him someplace. He wondered what had happened to Doris. He heard voices and he tried to see the people, to talk to them, but everything was black, and when he attempted to produce sound he only choked on the effort.

Well, wherever they were taking him, they sure were in a hurry. Maybe he was in very bad shape and it was one of those emergency deals. He wondered if it was broken bones or terrible burns or perhaps he had gone under a few times and there was a lot of water in his lungs. It felt like a combination of everything. There was ripping and cracking and burning and throbbing. There was the sound of gurgling and wheezing. There was the feeling of being slowly mashed between huge rubber rollers. The path of it all was down and up and very far down and high up and down again.

It was terribly far down on the last trip and it ended with a thud. Then everything was still, there was no noise. It lasted like that for a very long time.

Finally he was able to open his eyes.

He looked up at a ceiling of cracked plaster, split wide here and there to show the splintered wood supports. The walls were torn paper and the floor was wide, rough-surfaced beams, very old and very dirty. The light came from a single unshaded bulb hanging directly above his head. He couldn't understand why the light wasn't bothering his eyes. Just then the light blinded him and he winced and threw his arm across the upper part of his face.

He wondered where in the hell he was. Some pain jabbed at the back of his head and he let out a groan.

A voice said, "You're all right."

"Am I?" he said. "That's very interesting."

"You just got yourself a slight bump on the head."

He was able to recognize the voice. It belonged to Spann. But he didn't have the strength to sit up and look at Spann. He kept the arm across his face and with his other arm he reached down and felt the edge of the cot on which he was resting.

"You want anything?" Spann asked.

"Just tell me what happened."

"Mildred did it. She tagged you with something."

"You know what I think?" Cassidy said. "I think she fractured my skull."

"No," Spann murmured. "It ain't anything like that. It ain't bad at all."

Cassidy pulled himself up to a sitting position. He saw Spann seated on a shapeless and collapsed piece of furniture at the far end of the room.

"Where are we?" Cassidy asked.

"Upstairs," Spann said.

"Upstairs where?"

"Lundy's place."

Cassidy rubbed his fingers hard against his eyes. "Who brought me here?"

"Me and Shealy. That captain helped us get you off the ship. We carried you down Dock Street and up through the alley and got you in through the back door. How we did it without getting spotted, I don't know. But we did it."

"What do you want, a prize?"

"Lie down, Jim. Don't get yourself aggravated."

"I'd just like to know one thing. Who asked you bastards to butt in?"

"Aw, now look, if it wasn't for us—"

"If it wasn't for you I'd have been on that boat. With Doris. You hear me? We'd have been on our way to South Africa. Me and Doris."

"Go to sleep, Jim. We'll talk about it later."

Cassidy lowered his head to the pillow. An instant later he was sitting up and glaring at Spann and saying, "What time is it?"

"Two in the afternoon."

"Afternoon?" He looked up at the electric light. Then he jerked his head toward the window behind the cot, and he saw it was very dark outside. There was only a narrow gap between the window and the wall of the neighboring tenement, but the gap was thick with a strange, sullen darkness.

"It's another mean day," Spann said. "Any minute now it'll start coming down."

Cassidy continued to look out the window. "If it stays dark like this I'll make another try. I'll try another boat."

"You don't want to do that."

"Don't I?" He turned and glowered at Spann. "Tell me about it."

Spann stood up and came gliding toward the cot. He wore a faint smile. His long fingers played with a wide and thin cigarette case. He said, "You're a very important person. It's big headlines and they even got it on the radio. On the water front the cops are like flies. You can't turn your head without seeing a red car. If you walked out of here now I'd give a hundred to one they'd grab you inside of a minute."

Cassidy bit at the edge of his thumbnail. "That's nice to know."

"If you stay here," Spann said, "and if certain people keep their heads closed, there may be a chance for you."

"Who knows I'm here?"

"Me and Shealy. And Mildred and Pauline. And Lundy."

"What about Doris?"

Spann shrugged. "If you want me to tell her, I'll tell her.

119

But I think it's a mistake. I think what you better do is—"

"Give me a smoke."

Spann opened the thin case. They lit cigarettes. Spann took himself to the window and looked out, bent down to peer up past the tenement roofs to get a look at the sky. "Jesus Christ," he said, "it's gonna be something fierce. It's gonna be a cyclone."

"Good," Cassidy said. "I hope it's worse than that. I hope it's an earthquake."

Spann looked at him. "That ain't no way to talk."

"It's just the way I feel."

Spann came away from the window and blew a thick stream of smoke toward the floor. He flipped a thin forefinger along the smoke, cutting slices of it. He said, "You've slept a good nine hours. You ought to be hungry."

"Want to bring me something?"

"Sure," Spann said. "How would you like a nice bowl of stew?"

Cassidy shook his head. "No. Nothing to eat. Just get me a bottle of whisky."

He let his head drift back to the pillow and he heard Spann walking out and closing the door.

When he opened his eyes again it was an hour later and he saw that some furniture had been added to the room. There was a table and a few chairs. He saw them sitting at the table, Spann and Pauline and Shealy. They were sitting there and drinking quietly and he noticed there wasn't much left in the bottle.

For some unaccountable reason he didn't want them to know he was awake. He tried to probe the reason but it skipped away from him and it was playing with him, teasing him. He had his eyes closed and yet his full attention was aimed at the table.

He heard Shealy saying, "I don't know. Maybe I did wrong."

"I think you did," Pauline said.

Spann told Pauline to shut up.

"No," Pauline said. "I won't shut up, I say it was a rotten thing to do."

120

"You'll shut up," Spann told her, "or I'll reach inside your mouth and rip your tongue out."

Pauline said, "It's plain as day what'll happen now. We all know what'll happen. We know we can't trust Mildred. She's no good, she never was any good—"

"That isn't what bothers me," Shealy said.

"It should bother you," Pauline told him.

There was the sound of a chair scraping. Cassidy opened his eyes and saw Spann rising and Pauline rising. Spann aimed the heel of his palm at Pauline's face and Pauline leaned far back to get away, then came in very fast to collect a handful of Spann's hair. She pulled hard, and Spann opened his mouth wide and screamed without making a sound.

"Oh, stop it," Shealy said wearily. "Stop it, will you, please?"

Pauline let go and returned to her seat. Spann lowered his face into his hands and stayed that way for a few moments. Then he took a comb from his trousers pocket and combed his hair until it was flat and shining satiny across his head. He smiled sort of fondly at Pauline.

"Now the next time you do that," he told her, "I'm going to kill you. I'll get hold of your throat and I won't let go until you're dead."

Pauline was looking at Shealy and saying, "Sure it was a mistake. I can't understand why you didn't do what he asked you to do."

Shealy poured some whisky into a glass. He sent it down his throat and said, "I had my reasons. I'm beginning to think my reasons weren't good enough."

"Well, anyway," Pauline said, "you meant well."

"But I ruined it, didn't I?" Shealy's voice was dry and dragging and weary. "I ruined everything for him."

Spann said, "I think I'll go down and bring up another bottle."

"We could use another bottle," Shealy said.

Spann was at the door when Pauline said, "Bring a bottle of the special."

"That isn't for now." Spann was opening the door. "That's for later, when we can't taste it."

"I want it now," Pauline insisted. "I'm very much upset

121

and I need it now. Oh, God, look at Cassidy there. Look at poor Cassidy. Look at him, sound asleep. They'll find him, they'll snatch him, I know they will. Look at him, he wrecked the bus and killed twenty-six people—"

Spann came toward her and she grabbed the empty bottle and held it over her head.

"Put it down," Spann said.

Pauline lowered the bottle to the table. She sat down at the table and started to cry.

"Now, listen," Spann said gently to his girl friend. "You know better than to say a thing like that. You know it wasn't Cassidy's fault."

"What difference does that make?" Pauline cried. "The point is, he's getting the blame. They're looking for him. And they'll find him. And I hate to think what they'll give him."

Shealy's voice was down to a cracked whisper. "What do you think, Spann? What do you think he'll get?"

"It's hard to say. They can make it very stiff. After all, he broke away, he's on the loose. And another thing. Like it said in the papers. He's got that airplane crash on his record."

"What airplane crash?" Pauline asked.

"Didn't you know? He drove an airplane." Spann's tone was purely explanatory, as thought what he had just stated was only a fact and not part of a personal disaster.

Pauline was incredulous. "You mean Cassidy?"

"Sure," Spann said. "An airplane. One of them big jobs we see every day going back and forth up there. One of them great big silver jobs. He was the driver. Then in the paper it says how one day he's loaded when the plane takes off and instead of taking off it just folds up and lays down and starts to burn. So there's a lot of people killed. They put Cassidy on the grill and then after a while they let him go but it's on the record. You see what I mean? It's written there on the record."

"What else?" Pauline asked.

"On the record?"

"No," Pauline said. "Just about Cassidy. What else about Cassidy?"

"She means the good things," Shealy said to Spann. "The good things that they don't put on the record. The brighter side of the picture, like his family and where he went to school, and what college he attended."

"College?" Spann said. "Did he tell you he went to college?"

"No," Shealy replied. "He never mentioned a thing about it. But I'll wager that I'm correct. He has a college education."

"He sure don't talk like it," Spann murmured.

"I'll tell you why," Shealy said. "He's been through a certain process. It's something on the order of oxidation. When the bright polish comes off and for a while there's only the dull surface and then slowly it arrives, the rust. It's a special kind of rust. It gets under the surface and goes way down deep."

"Will you do me a favor?" Pauline said to Shealy. "Will you please tell me what it is you're talking about?"

"We're talking about Cassidy," Spann said.

"I didn't ask you, you lizard. All I asked you was go downstairs and bring up a bottle."

Cassidy was flat on his back on the cot, feeling the stabbing burning of the pain that was now acute in his skull. He had his head turned slightly so that he was afforded a full view of them at the table. He saw Spann moving toward the door, opening the door and walking out. Then Pauline got up from the table and approached the cot. Cassidy's eyes were closed again.

"Look at him," Pauline said. "Look at this poor devil."

He could feel the pressure of Pauline's eyes looking down at him with sympathy, the pure kind, the kind that wasn't embroidered.

"They'll catch him," Pauline moaned. "I know they'll catch him. Oh, God, they'll put him away for a hundred years."

"Not that long," Shealy said.

"How long?" Her voice aimed at the table. "Tell me, Shealy. What's the rap on a deal like that?"

"Spann knows more about it than I do."

"Spann was never up for that. Spann was up for forgery

and embezzlement. For passing bad checks and mail fraud. He was up for—well, he was up for a lot of things. But never anything like this. This is something altogether different. For God's sake, look what's happening to this poor man. He's gonna be held for mass murder."

"I wish you'd sit down and be quiet for a while." Shealy sounded as though he were in pain. "You're not helping me any."

"Helping you?" Pauline's voice was brittle. "What do you mean, helping you?"

"Good Christ," Sliealy groaned. "What did I do? What did I do?"

"I'll tell you what you did." Now her voice climbed and became harsh and unmerciful. "You took your good friend Cassidy and sent him on a trip straight up the creek. You even admit it. You said you made him a promise. You promised him you'd bring Doris to that boat—"

"But I knew—"

"You knew too much. You always know too much. You go around telling people what you know. But here's what I think, Shealy. I think you're slaphappy. Now how do you like that?"

"I don't like it. But I'm afraid it's true."

"You're goddamn right it's true. You're just a slaphappy old soak. You can't no longer weigh yourself in terms of pounds. Now it's in terms of quarts. And another thing—"

"Oh, please. please, Pauline—"

"Please nothing. I say what I think. I ain't no hypocrite. Look at that man over there on the cot. Just look at him. I tell you my heart bleeds for that man. I can see them sending him up for twenty, thirty years—"

"Maybe we can—"

"There ain't a thing we can do and you know it. You had a chance to help him, Shealy. You had a wonderful chance to really do something for him. And for Doris. Yeah, for him and Doris. For the two of them."

Shealy lowered his head to the table.

"But no," Pauline said. "Instead of helping them, what did you do? Instead of telling Doris where he was, who did you tell? You told that filthy tramp, that mud hen with the

124

big mouth, that sloppy thing who has the colossal gall to say that she's married to him."

"But they are married," Shealy groaned. "They're man and wife."

"On what basis?" she demanded. "Because someone got paid to stand in front of them and read some lines? Because Cassidy went out and bought a ring? You telling me that made it sacred? That put a blessing on it? I don't see it that way. I see it the other way. I claim that Cassidy was cursed. Yes, goddamnit, I say she put a curse on him."

Shealy raised his head slightly. "You say that because you hate Mildred. You envy her. She's got the looks."

"Looks?" It was a screech. "If that's what they call looks, I'll stay thin as a rail and I'll make myself get thinner. I'll live on water and dry figs. You see these things I got up front? They're little, aren't they? They hardly show. But I'll tell you what they can do. They can hit my boy friend Spann like bullets shot from a gun. They hit him and he staggers and he gets dry in the mouth. He looks at them and he gulps like he's choking on something. But then when I give it to Spann I give it to keep him alive, like he's my baby and I'm feeding him. And sometimes I cry, I cry real soft but there's tears. And I whisper in his ear. I say, Spann you're evil, you're a lizard. But you're my baby."

"If it's that way," Shealy said, "if you have that, you shouldn't envy anybody."

Pauline didn't hear him. "Yes," she stated emphatically. "Of course I'm thin. After all, that's the fashion. To be like a straw, like a reed. To be slender like you see them in the magazines advertising the dresses. To be like that. Built like that. Not like a goddamn battleship."

"Then I was right," Shealy murmured. "You do envy her."

It was quiet and Pauline was lowering herself into a chair at the table. Finally Pauline said, "I'm sick. That's why I'm so skinny. I'm skinny and I'm sick. But Mildred? She's healthy. Why is it the meaner they are, the healthier they are?"

Shealy rested his chin on his folded arms on the table. He peered up at Pauline and said nothing.

She answered her own question. "I'll tell you why," she said. "Because they're always taking. Like bloodsuckers."

"No," Shealy said. "Not Mildred."

Pauline leaped up and banged her bony fist against the table. "I say yes," she cried. "I call her a rotten bloodsucker."

"You know nothing about it."

"More than you, Shealy. A lot more than you." She beat her fist against the table. She started to cry.

Cassidy had his eyes half-opened. He noticed that the light from the electric bulb was more intensified, which meant it was getting darker outside. It was going to be a big storm. Very nice weather for April, he remarked to himself. Another series of pains started shooting back and forth inside his head and he decided it must be something serious. If it wasn't a skull fracture it was probably a bad concussion. Or maybe he had some kind of a hemorrhage in there. He told himself it really didn't matter too much. But it would be nice if Doris was here. No, that wasn't what he meant. He meant it would be nice if he wasn't here, if he was somewhere far away with Doris. And it could have been that way. They could have been on the boat together. Well, it was too bad. But all at once he wasn't thinking about that. He was listening to Pauline.

Pauline was saying, "I ought to know all about it. I lost out." She inhaled deeply and it made a grinding sound and then it was a quivering sob. "I remember the way it was, it was four years ago, that day when Cassidy came walking into Lundy's. A lot of us girls were there and right away we were looking at him. Me especially because Spann was doing a stretch and I'd been without it for months and months. So I'm sitting there and I see that thick curly blond hair and that big fine chest and all that solid muscle beef, all that fine man."

"Oh, stop it," Shealy said. "You've been drinking all last night and all today and now you're drawing pictures."

"Am I? It's a picture that happened. The way I'm sitting there, hoping he'll see me. I tell you I kept crossing my legs and lighting cigarettes, just hoping he'd notice me. But no. Instead he notices something sitting at a table. He sees a great big pair of cantaloupes sticking out from under a blouse."

"Forget that."

"I was sitting there lighting cigarettes. I weighed ninety-two pounds."

"It was a long time ago," Shealy said.

"It was four years ago and I sat there and I saw them walk out. I went to my room and I wrote a long letter to Spann. Then I read it and I tore it up."

"All right," Shealy said. "All right."

"But let me tell you. Will you let me tell you? It was after Mildred got him to marry her. That was when I got the other feeling. I mean, just feeling sorry for him. Maybe just wanting to touch the fuzzy gold hair on his thick wrist, or give him a very light kiss on the side of his face. Maybe knit him a pair of socks or something like that. Like going to his room just to see that his bed was made and he had a clean sheet to sleep on. To cook him a decent meal because I'm ready to swear she never did that for him. I remember once in the winter he had a bad cold and he treated it here, right here in Lundy's Place. His throat was so bad he could hardly talk and he stood at the bar and drank glass after glass of rock-and-rye until it made him damn good and sick and he threw up. And where was his wife? I'll tell you where she was. She was having herself a time in China-town. At one of those places where they play fan-tan and drink some rice slop."

"You mean rice wine. It's good. I've tasted it."

"His wife. How can you sit there and say it? How can you say she's ever been his wife? What did she ever do for him? What did she ever give him? I'll tell you what she gave him. Pure hell."

The door opened and Spann came in carrying a bottle of colorless liquor. He opened the bottle and Pauline extended a water glass and he filled it for her. Then he filled Shealy's glass. He poured the equivalent of a jigger into his own glass.

Pauline raised her glass and took several long gulps. She banged the half-empty glass on the table and turned to Shealy and said, "So that's what you did. Instead of telling Doris where he was, you told his wife."

Spann circled the table and came toward Pauline and said, "Are you still at it?"

"I want him to know what he's done." She lifted her glass to her lips and took another long gulp. "Shealy, it's only that I've known you for so long. It's only that I'm so fond of you. If it wasn't for that, I'd take the bottle and smash it across your face."

Shealy got up from the table, crossed the room and opened the door and walked out.

"That just about does it," Spann said gently. He lowered his head, as though he was bowing to Pauline. And he took her wrist, as though he meant to kiss the back of her hand. He bit hard into the back of her hand, and Pauline shrieked and jerked her hand away.

"Look what you did," she said, indicating the teeth marks on her hand. "Look, look!"

"I told you to leave Shealy alone. Why do you drill away at people?"

"Look what you did to my hand."

"That's only a sample. You start with Shealy again and I'll give you the rest of it."

"Give it to me now," Pauline said. She backed away so that the table was between herself and Spann.

"Come on, give it to me now."

Spann started to turn his back to her and she reached down and picked up the bottle and threw it at him. It barely missed him and he stood still and watched it crashing against the wall.

"Come on," Pauline said. "Come on, lizard."

Spann's small, slim body went flashing around the table and then, like a tiny animal making a precise attack, he flew to Pauline's side and he had her arm and he was biting at the upper part of it. Pauline shrieked again and struggled to break away.

"Oh, Mother," she shrieked. "Oh, Jesus."

She quivered and shrieked very loudly as she rolled her head and stood there allowing Spann to bite away at her arm.

"Biting me," she sang out at the top of her voice. "Look

128

what he's doing. He's biting me to death. Why, just look at him, will you? He's biting my arm off."

Then for a moment she was an interested spectator watching Spann as he bit away at the upper part of a woman's arm. Her eyes widened slightly, then suddenly closed and were shut tightly, and with her other arm she pistoned her fist against Spann's forehead. Spann's teeth were parted and he sailed back, collided with a chair, and landed on his side. Pauline had another chair in her hands and she was raising the chair, aiming it at Spann. He crouched there on the floor, his arms in front of his face. Without a sound he was begging her not to throw the chair. She raised the chair higher. Then she hurled the chair at Spann and he was darting to one side, but he wasn't fast enough. The chair caught him in the ribs and he made a sound something like a howling dog. He howled again as Pauline ran at him. He went on howling as he rolled across the floor, evading her clutching fingers.

She had him for an instant, but he broke away and raced to the door and opened it and scampered out.

Pauline fell to her knees. She shook her fist at the door. She opened her mouth very wide and sobbed wheezingly. She stretched herself out so that she was flat face-down on the floor and she beat her fists against the splintered wood. She went on doing that until a noise from across the room caused her to raise her head.

The noise was made by the springs of the cot as Cassidy slowly sat up.

Pauline stared at him and moaned, "Oh, Mother."

"Get me a drink," Cassidy said. He frowned at her while she got up off the floor. "Go on, go downstairs and bring me a bottle. And not that white rotgut, either. I want rye whisky."

Pauline smiled brightly. She wiped her hands across her tear-stained face.

"Tell Lundy to charge it," Cassidy said. Then he remembered the roll of bills in his trousers pocket. He reached under the thin blanket, and discovered he wasn't wearing the trousers. He was wearing only his cotton shorts.

Pauline hurried out of the room. Cassidy sat stiffly

upright in the cot, wondering what they had done with his pants. Goddamnit, he had something like eighty dollars in those pants. His lips were very tight, clamped grimly as he told himself he needed that eighty dollars, it was all he had. Suddenly he was aware of something more important than the money. The bad pain had gone away and now there was only a dull ache and it, too, seemed to be subsiding. He could feel the balance and the clarity returning to his head. He reached up and back and felt the bump on his skull. It pained sharply when he touched it, but that was only the bruise and it didn't go any deeper than that. It was dry and he knew the skin hadn't been broken and it was just a bad bump on the head, that was all.

The door opened and Pauline came in with a bottle of rye whisky and a pack of cigarettes. She lit two cigarettes and filled two water glasses almost to the top. She pulled a chair toward the cot and sat down and gave Cassidy his smoke and his drink.

Cassidy sipped the whisky and shook his head. "Pauline, I hate to bother you again but I want some water. My stomach's empty and I'll need a chaser."

"Why, certainly, honey. By all means." She ran out of the room and came back with a glass of water.

"Thanks," Cassidy said. He took a long but rapid drink of the rye whisky.

Pauline smiled at him. "Now drink your water, honey. Drink it down."

He gulped some water. Then he repeated it with the whisky and the water. He dragged at the cigarette, inhaling very deeply and letting the smoke come out slowly. He grinned at Pauline and said, "Now I feel better."

"Oh, that's wonderful, honey. That's just wonderful."

He drank some more whisky.

Pauline said, "Now look, honey, if there's anything you want me to do, just tell me. Anything at all."

"Just sit here," he said. "Just sit here and drink with me."

They lifted their glasses and looked at each other while they drank.

Then there was the sudden crackle of angry electricity in the sky and Pauline gave a little scream. Cassidy turned fast and stared at the window. He saw it was almost pitch-black out there. The high crackling sound came again and beyond it, like a bass effect, there was the dull booming noise.

"Here," Pauline said. "Here's another drink."

She was filling his glass again. She handed it to him and refilled her own glass.

Cassidy gulped some whisky and chased it with the water. He lifted the glass of whisky to take another drink and then he noticed the way Pauline was sitting there and looking at him. Her very thin and very white face was whiter than usual, and her eyes were extremely sharp and bright.

She said, "Don't get the wrong notion. It ain't that I don't want Spann. I guess I'll always want Spann."

Cassidy lowered the glass to the floor. He lit another cigarette.

"But then," Pauline said, "if you wanted to take me away from Spann, I think you could do it."

He grinned at her. He twisted the grin and shook his head.

"Well, anyway," she said, "you could try."

There was another crackling banging booming in the air high above Lundy's Place, and Pauline shivered violently and spilled some whisky on the blanket over Cassidy's legs.

"Oh, God," she said. "Oh, Jesus."

"It's only the weather." He reached across the bed and put his hand on her shoulder to steady her.

But she went on shivering and her lips quivered. "Listen to it. When it sounds like that it scares the life out of me. It makes me think it's the end of the world."

"Maybe it is."

"Oh, no," she said very fast. "Oh, no. Cassidy, please don't say that."

"But then, suppose it is. What's the difference?"

"Oh, for God's sake. Oh, please, honey, you mustn't talk like that. Oh, please, please." She was spilling whisky on the blanket, then allowing the glass to roll down toward the edge of the cot. She was starting to weep again. She wrapped her arms around the blanket where it covered Cassidy's legs. She was hugging his legs and working her way toward his knees, then past his knees.

He caught her wrists and said, "Hey, where you going?"

"You gotta believe me. It ain't that I don't want Spann."

"Then what do you want?"

"Can't we just have a session? Just once?"

"No," he said. He felt sorry for her and there was no way for him to say it or show it, so he said angrily, "If you can't hold your whisky better than that, get the hell out of here."

"Honey, I'm not drunk. Don't be sore at me."

"All right then. Cut it out. Behave yourself."

"Look at me, I'm crying. Look how shaky I am. I guess it's a lot of things. Seeing you here like this. All banged up with a bump on the head and not being able to move out of this room. Hiding up here like an animal. Listen, honey, I have to tell you this. You don't have a chance. I know you don't. Don't you see? I only want to do something for you, make you feel better."

He released her wrists. She put her hands against his ribs and he sat there and allowed her to do that. She wrapped her arms around his middle and lowered her head so that it rested against his side. He patted her head and with his other hand he reached over the side of the cot, lifted the whisky glass, and took a gulp. Pauline turned her head and he gave her some of the whisky.

"There," he said. "How's that?"

"Oh, honey." She raised herself a little so that she was trying to press all her weight against his chest. "It's such a rotten life. Sometimes I'd give anything just to be dead. Look at what they're doing to you. A fine sweet honest man and, yes, I mean that, I mean it from the heart. And that's where it hurts me because I know they'll put you away for years, and years, and years. The dirty bastards. All of then."

He gazed past her head and saw the torn wallpaper across the room. He said, "You're a good friend."

"And you, honey," she said. "You stand aces high with me. You always did."

They were smiling fondly at each other and he said, "You're not sore at me?"

"Why should I be sore?"

"Well, I said no."

"Ah, honey, that's all right. I'm glad you said no. I guess I just got worked up for a minute. Now I'm calmed down. But still I wish there was some way I could help you."

Just then the walls seemed to groan and shudder and from outside there was a tremendous crash and rumbling and another crash and a flare of blue-white came blazing into the room.

"Oh, Mother," she gasped.

Cassidy took hold of her shoulders. "Listen," he said. "There is a way you can help me. I want you to go find Doris."

She was staring at the window. "Doris?"

"Find her and bring her up here."

"When?"

"Now," he said. "If you go now you won't get caught in the rain."

Pauline took her eyes away from the window. She looked at Cassidy and nodded seriously and said, "That's right. I'll go and I'll find Doris and I'll bring her here. Because this is where she should be. With you. You're absolutely right."

"Then go," he said. "Hurry."

And he shoved her gently away from the cot and saw her walking toward the door. But then he wasn't looking at her. He was looking at the door as it opened and Mildred came in.

Pauline was startled by the abruptness of Mildred's entrance and let out a little cry and veered to one side. Then she darted toward the door, trying to get past Mildred.

"What's the rush?" Mildred said. She took a backward step and blocked Pauline's path to the door.

"Let me out," Pauline said.

Mildred was looking at Cassidy. "What's going on?"

"What's that to you?" Pauline screeched. "Who asked you to come in?"

Mildred turned her head slightly and frowned at Pauline. "Why? Wasn't I supposed to come in?"

Instead of replying, Pauline made another attempt to reach the door. Mildred caught her around the waist, raised an elbow to hold her there, bent back. Pauline began to struggle

133

and Mildred tightened the hold. Her elbow pressed against Pauline's chin. Pauline's head was bent far back.

"Just answer me," Mildred said to Pauline. "Just tell me what was going on."

Pauline tried to speak but the pressure against her chin prevented her from moving her jaws.

Cassidy said, "Let go of her."

"I'll break her goddamned neck," Mildred said. She gave a sort of jab with the elbow, and Pauline fell back and sat down hard on the floor.

Cassidy rolled himself off the cot and started toward Mildred. She stood there waiting for him, her hands on her hips, her feet planted wide, bracing herself, all set for him.

He turned away from Mildred and focused his attention on Pauline. He was helping Pauline to get up from the floor. Pauline had sat down very hard and she had a thoughtful, somewhat worried look as she reached back to rub her thinly upholstered behind.

"Hey, now," she said. "It feels like it's fractured."

But then she saw Mildred standing there and instantly she forgot everything but the animosity she felt for Mildred. Her eyes narrowed and she smiled a thin and vicious smile and said to Mildred, "Please forgive me. I should have told you. Your husband was sending me out on an errand."

Mildred didn't budge. "What kind of errand?"

Pauline widened the smile. "He wants Doris."

It was quiet for a few moments and then Mildred said, "All right, dearie. That's all right with me." She stepped aside, giving Pauline a clear path to the door. "Go ahead. Go bring Doris."

The smile faded from Pauline's lips and her eyes began to widen. She walked out of the room and closed the door.

Cassidy went to the cot and sat down on the edge of it. He lit a cigarette and as he took the first long puff he was hearing another extended crash of thunder. He turned his head and looked out the window and saw the first big drops coming down. Then there were more drops and faster and faster and louder and then it was really coming down.

He heard Mildred saying, "I guess she won't bring Doris. She'd be crazy to go out in that rain. Look at the way it's raining."

He kept his eyes on the window. He watched the torrent of the slashing rain.

Then his voice was part of the torrent, with the force of it and the tremor of it as he said, "I don't know why you're here, but I'm waiting here for Doris. When Doris comes, I'm throwing you out."

Chapter Thirteen

He expected her to reply immediately, and he braced himself for what he thought would be a violent reaction. Instead, it was quiet in the room and the quiet seemed to be heavier than the sound of the storm outside. Then, after a while, he heard the tinkling of a bottle against a glass. He turned away from the window and looked toward the center of the room.

Mildred was sitting at the table. She was pouring herself a stiff drink. She was sitting there comfortably with the drink and a cigarette. She was bent forward just a little so that her plump elbows were on the table, her tremendous breasts jutting out like a shelf above the table, her back slanting down straight along the spine until it made the start of the big bold swirling roundness, very heavy, very round, balanced with the rest of her, the brazen luscious roundness.

She saw Cassidy looking at her, and she bent further forward and twisted her body just a little so that she was effectively displaying the slimness of her waist in contrast to the big bulging roundness up front and in back. Then, very slowly, she lifted an arm and let her fingers sink deeply into the thick mass of her black hair, and with her other arm she sort of played around along the top of her blouse. Gradually the buttons up there were slipping out of the buttonholes. She bent over just a little more and it showed the massive thrust of her breasts, bared very low and trying to burst away from the edge of the brassiere.

Cassidy turned his back to her and walked over to the cot. He stood at the edge of the cot, looking down at the rumpled blanket. He heard the soft, almost imperceptible sound of rustling fabric. It was entirely apart from the sound of the storm outside. In his ears it became a loud sound.

He pivoted and moved toward the table, not looking at Mildred. His eyes aimed at the bottle and the glasses and the cigarettes. He was at the table and pouring a drink. He heard the sound of something soft hitting the floor, and he looked at the floor and saw her blouse.

Again he turned away from the table. He carried his drink and his cigarette to the cot and sat down at the end of the cot so that he was facing the door. He put the glass of whisky on the floor and took a few puffs at the cigarette, then slowly lowered his hand toward the glass, lifted the glass to his hips and was starting to drink the whisky when he heard the metallic sound of a zipper being opened. He spilled some of the whisky on his chin.

Then there was the somewhat thick and definite sound of the skirt sliding down past the hips. The sound of the storm came crashing through, seemed to recede to allow the sounds in the room to become dominant, then crashed through again, then receded again. Cassidy started to turn his eyes toward the center of the room, jerked his head back to force his eyes toward the door, toward the floor, toward anywhere except the table. But just then something bright purple came sailing past his eyes and fell on the floor at his feet.

He looked at it. The bright purple was her favorite color and she had a habit of dyeing all her underclothes a bright and bold shade of purple. The rayon slip at his feet was an extremely bright purple and as he looked at it, it seemed to be on fire. The purple blaze of it came flaring up into his eyes and he winced and bit hard at his lip. He looked at the glass of whisky in his hand and suddenly it seemed that something was happening to the whisky. The color of the whisky was bright purple.

Cassidy stood up and hurled the glass of whisky at the

136

door. There was the sound of breaking glass, but it was only a small sound because just then a crash of thunder jarred the room.

The electric light went out.

He gazed up in the complete darkness, trying to estimate where the bulb would be. Maybe the bulb needed tightening. He reached up and moved his hand back and forth and couldn't feel the bulb or the wire. He lowered his arm and stepped backward toward the center of the room. There was another crashing booming sound from the storm outside and then the light suddenly came on again.

The edge of the table seemed to be pressing against his back. He was facing the window. It was like a weird kind of mirror made out of black glass, with little pools of water running wild all over it. But against the wet black there was a white shimmer, and then against the white there was the bright purple. He had his hands gripping the edge of the table as he stared at the window and saw the movement of the bright purple. It was coming up and out and away from the white.

He heard it as it landed on the floor. He looked down and saw the bright purple brassiere on the floor.

His hands came away from the edge of the table. He was moving slowly toward the cot. He told himself to get in under the blanket and close his eyes and try to go to sleep. He climbed onto the cot and started to pull the blanket over his legs and toward his shoulders. There was a sound from the center of the room. It was the sound of wood scraping against the floor as a chair was pushed back.

Cassidy tossed the blanket off the cot and threw his legs over the side. He started to rise from the edge of the cot, but he saw something in front of him that caused him to blink, caused him to bounce back onto the cot. It was as though he had been hit in the chest with a sledge hammer.

He saw Mildred standing there in the center of the room: She wore shoes and stockings and a bright purple girdle. Her hands were cupped against the swirl of her hips. Her breasts were high up and all the way out and the nipples seemed to be precisely aimed.

137

Mildred said, "Come here."

He tried to drag his eyes away from her. He couldn't do it.

"Come here," she said. "I want to tell you something."

Her voice was soft and rich and thick. Like thick taffy. She smiled and took a step toward him.

"Keep away," he said.

"What's the matter?" she asked easily with the taffy voice. "Don't you like what you're looking at?"

"I've seen it before."

She raised her hands to her breasts. She cupped her hands under her breasts and tested the fullness and the weight of them. "They're heavier now than they've ever been. Aren't they gorgeous?"

He felt as though he was being choked. "You cheap tramp."

"But look at them."

"You know what I ought to do? I ought to—"

"Come on, look at them," she said.

He told himself it shouldn't be difficult. It was just a matter of taking his mind away from what he was seeing, and thinking solely in terms of what a scum she was.

He leaned back on the cot, resting on his elbows, inclined his head somewhat judiciously, and said, "Yeah, they're not bad." He allowed his eyes to give her an idea of what he was going to say. His eyes were brutal. "We ought to get together sometime. What price do you charge?"

Either it didn't get across or if it did get across she was letting it ride. She didn't say anything. She took another step toward him.

The muscles in his jaws moved in and out. "I guess it don't do no good to call you names. I guess the only thing for me to do is slap you down."

She smiled thickly, lushly, her lower lip full and gleaming. She said, "You won't do that."

Then, sort of flowing, not fast and yet suddenly, not violently and yet with an aggressiveness that dominated the moment, she moved in on him and had her arms around his neck as she sat herself on his lap. She placed her lips against his mouth, and they were full and moist with the thick velvety warmth that became warmer. Then it was very warm and presently it was wet fire.

He heard the whisper that had a blade in it. "You still want that other woman?"

It was so very slow and yet with the powerful surge, the way she had her weight pressing against him, the presence of her hands at the sides of his face as her lips kissed the fire into him, and then the way her fingers crawled up past his temples and into his hair and squirmed there, and writhed.

"You still want Doris?"

She had him now so that his shoulders were flat upon the blanket. He looked up and saw the black flame of her eyes. He realized suddenly that his hands were on her and he told himself to stop it and make her stop it. He tried to take his hands away, but his hands refused to let go. Then his arms were wrapped around her middle and he was rolling her over, but not all the way because she was doing something with her mouth on his mouth that caused him to stop moving and sort of drove him crazy.

"Well?" she breathed. "You still want her? You sure?"

Then there was more of what she was doing. Then there was something else. And there was more of that. He heard the mixture of clicking and thudding as she kicked her shoes off her feet and they hit the floor. The sound was magnified in his ears and it drilled its way through his brain. It was echoed and echoed again. It was the echo of all the times she had kicked her shoes off while they were in the bed together and it was raining outside.

"You wanna do something?" Her voice was low and husky and the color of it was dark purple. "Wouldja like to take off my girdle?"

He put his hands on the band of elastic around her waist.

"Do it slow," she said.

He started to pull the girdle down past her thighs.

"Slower," she said. "I wantcha to do it real slow. Do it nice."

He lowered the girdle very slowly and got it down to her ankles. He slipped it past her ankles and let it fall to the floor. Then he was sitting up and looking down at her as she rested there on her back, smiling up at him. He bent his head toward the spicy richness of her bulging breasts.

"Take them," she breathed, her eyes half-closed, but with the glitter coming through the lashes.

Then it was all the richness and the wild spice and it went on until suddenly something was pushing him away. He had no idea of what was pushing him away. It was something tangible and he could certainly feel it, but he couldn't accept the truth of it. He just couldn't believe that her hands were on his chest and she was pushing him away.

"What is it?" he mumbled.

"Get up."

"What for?"

"Just like that."

He tried to put his brain in gear. "Like what?" Now he knew she really meant it. She wasn't playing, she was really pushing him away.

She shoved him firmly and rolled herself toward the other side of the cot. Then she got up off the cot and walked around it and she was moving toward the table in the center of the room. She picked up the pack of cigarettes and took one out. She put the cigarette in her mouth and struck a match.

As the match flared she turned and smiled at Cassidy through the flame. She inhaled deeply and as the smoke came out of her mouth, she said, "Let me have my girdle."

He stared down at the floor and saw the bright purple girdle. He reached down slowly and had it in his hand. "Should I bring it to you?"

"Just let me have it."

"I think you want me to bring it to you," he said. "You want me to crawl over there on my hands and knees."

She stood there smoking the cigarette.

"That's what you want," Cassidy said. "You want me to crawl."

She didn't reply. She took a long drag at the cigarette and blew the smoke toward Cassidy.

He watched the smoke drifting in, saw her there on the other side of the smoke. The bright purple girdle was something blazing hot in his hand and he hurled the girdle across the room so that it struck a wall and dropped to the floor.

"I ain't crawling," Cassidy said.

But saying it wasn't enough. He knew he had to do something to prevent himself from crawling. He was staggered, reeling and dizzy and almost knocked senseless with the need to have her now, right now. There was nothing else, there was only the need. He told himself she had said no, she had pushed him away. For a flashing instant it wasn't himself who was being pushed away, it was Haney Kenrick and she was shaking her head and saying no, no. But then again it was Cassidy. She was saying no to Cassidy.

"The hell you say," he growled, and he was up from the cot and lunging at her. She let him come close and then she jabbed at him with her fingernails. He didn't feel it. She sent the lighted cigarette against his bare chest and he didn't feel it. She scratched him again, she was punching and kicking but he didn't feel any of it, he was lifting her off the floor, lifting her high. He threw her down flat on the cot. She tried to get up and he pushed her down. Again she tried to get up and he put his hand on her face and pushed her down. She tried to bite his hand and he took it away from her face and then his hands were on her wrists. She fought and fought, but his knees pushed hard against her thighs. She screamed and her screams clashed with the roaring of the storm and the wild clatter of the rain. Then it was all one sound. It was raging thunder.

Chapter Fourteen

Cassidy worked his face deeper into the pillow. He heard the voice again and then he felt the hand on his shoulder. He knew he was being robbed of sleep that he needed very much. He had been sleeping for many hours but still it wasn't enough and he was aching for more sleep. Somewhat dimly he remembered what had happened with Mildred, and he knew that was why he needed all this sleep. He told himself he ought to sleep for twelve or fourteen hours.

141

"Come on, get up," Pauline said. "I brought you up something to eat."

He kept his eyes closed. "What time is it?"

"Around ten-thirty." She tugged at his shoulder. "It's ten-thirty at night and it's time you had some food in your stomach."

He opened his eyes and sat up. He blinked and grinned dazedly at Pauline. Then he looked past her and saw the tray on the table. He started to get out of bed and remembered he had nothing on.

"Where's all my clothes?"

"There's your shirt, on a chair. Your shorts are on the floor."

"Listen," he said. "I want the rest of my clothes. I want my pants and I want my shoes."

"They're downstairs."

"Get them."

She touched her fingers to her lips in a little worried gesture. "Shealy said if you had all your clothes you'd get dressed and walk out. And you mustn't walk out. Shealy said you've got to stay here. And Spann said—"

"What's the matter, Pauline? You afraid of Spann?"

Her attitude changed. She tossed her head arrogantly. "Now, you know better than that. If Spann starts anything with me I'll throw him on the floor and kick him."

"Good," he said. "That's fine. Now get me my clothes."

She made a move toward the door and then she stopped and looked at him and said, "I'll hide the clothes under a blanket. I'll tell them you said it got chilly in here and you wanted another blanket."

Cassidy didn't reply. He waited until she had walked out and then he slipped into the shorts and put on the shirt. He went to the table to see what was on the tray. There was a bowl of lamb stew and some bread and butter. The stew looked good and a lot of steam was coming up from it. He realized he was very hungry and this appeared to be a bowl of very fine stew. There was considerable meat in it and the gravy was thick with vegetables. He told himself to sit down and enjoy the stew. Later he would think about the situation and he would plan the getaway. But he would do that later and right now the big thing was this bowl of lamb stew.

He sat down at the table and started to eat. He told himself it was a wonderful stew. The only food that Lundy served downstairs was lamb stew or beef stew or pickled pigs' feet that came in jars. Sometimes Lundy would go out in a boat on Sundays and then on Mondays he would offer hard-shell crabs at a dime apiece and they would go very fast. But that was in the summertime when the hard-shell crabs were running. Last summer Lundy had invited him to go out in the boat, and now it was sort of pleasant to remember that Sunday when he and Shealy and Spann and Lundy were out in the rowboat looking for hard-shell crabs. They had the fish heads to entice the crabs and then when the crabs became voracious and really went for the fish heads, they scooped up the crabs with hand nets. That had been a really fine Sunday. That night they came back to Lundy's Place and ate up every damn crab and between the four of them they must have finished twelve or fourteen quarts of beer. Then Lundy really lost control of himself and handed out cigars. They all leaned back in their chairs with the cigars and their bellies loaded up with blue-claw crabmeat and beer, and they smoked their cigars and talked about crabbing and fishing. That had sure been a fine Sunday.

There weren't many fine Sundays to remember. There were a few half-decent Sundays when he would go over to the park and watch the kids playing. He'd sit there alone on a bench and the kids would be playing and he'd buy some candy and distribute it. Sooner or later they would have him in a conversation and they would tell him all about themselves and their mommies and daddies and brothers and sisters. They were four- and five- and six-year-old kids who belonged to very large and very poor families, and most of the time they were in the park unattended, except for some older brother or sister who sat reading a comic book and paying no attention to them. It was pleasant to talk to the kids but then after a while it became somewhat difficult because he would be thinking that he had no children of his own, and it was a vacant, sort of dismal feeling. At the same time it was a damn good thing he and Mildred didn't have any children. He was always telling Mildred she'd better take special care not to get herself started, and she was always telling him he shouldn't worry his head about it, she sure as hell didn't want to be bothered with brats.

That was why most of the Sundays had been downright miserable. That kind of talk. That kind of atmosphere. It was always that way after they were out of bed and getting dressed. When they were moving around in the small rooms of the flat and getting in each other's way. And yet, come to think of it—

No, he said to himself. He wasn't going to think of it. He wasn't going to think of anything until he had finished this bowl of lamb stew and the bread and butter. And certainly, when he was finished with the meal, he wasn't going to needle himself with thinking about the past. The thing to do was figure a plan for getting out of here tonight and out of the city before morning. And with Doris. Yes, damnit, with Doris. He wondered why he had to emphasize it to himself. It ought to come easily, like saying he and Doris would be leaving town tonight. Like that, automatically.

The door opened and Pauline came in carrying a folded blanket. As she approached the table she was unfolding the blanket and he saw his trousers and his shoes. He stopped eating long enough to put on the trousers and shoes, and he saw Pauline sitting down across the table and looking at him worriedly.

He dipped the spoon into the stew, took a big mouthful, crammed bread into his mouth and frowned at Pauline.

He swallowed the stew and the bread and said, "What's bothering you?"

"Your clothes, I don't think I should have done it."

He went back to the stew. He took a final spoonful, used the last chunk of bread to wipe the bowl clean, then swallowed the bread and took a drink of water. He lit a cigarette and gave one to Pauline and lit it for her.

"Now, look," he said. "All you're doing is helping me."

"But Shealy said—"

"The hell with what Shealy said. Look at the way Shealy loused things up. Why, if it wasn't for Shealy, I'd have been in good shape."

"I know that."

"Well?"

"Well," she said, "at the same time maybe it's good to look at this thing from more than one angle—"

"That isn't you talking," he cut in. "That's Shealy. That's the outside advice I don't want and I don't need."

"But, honey—"

"But nothing."

"Look, honey. They're trying to work something out. They're keeping you here for your own good."

"Nobody's keeping me anywhere." He stood up. He didn't like the way she was looking at him, the way she was slowly shaking her head.

He turned away from the table and listened to the noise from outside. It was the dull persistence of the rain, the steady downpour that he knew would go on all night and probably all next day.

He gazed morosely at the window. "This afternoon I asked you to do something for me. You said you would."

He waited for a reply.

Then he said, "I sent you out to look for Doris."

Again he waited.

He turned and glared at Pauline. "Well? What happened? Did you find her?"

"Sure."

"Whaddya mean sure? Why didn't you bring her up here?"

"I did," Pauline said.

He threw his hand toward the side of his face. He pressed his fingers hard against his temple.

Pauline tightened the side of her mouth. "Should I give you the picture?"

"No," he said. "I can see the picture."

He could see the door opening and Pauline and Doris coming into the room. And Doris standing there in the doorway, looking at Mildred and him sleeping together on the cot.

"Don't feel bad about it," Pauline said. "Doris didn't mind."

He took a step backward. "What do you mean, she didn't mind?"

"She was dead drunk. She was five miles high."

So then he could see Pauline taking Doris by the arm and backing out of the room and quietly closing the door. He could see the cot with Mildred and him sleeping together and then after a while Mildred waking up and getting dressed and going out. He wondered how she had the strength to lift herself out of the cot. He sure had delivered it to her. He was some man, he was. He had looked at a pair of naked breasts and had told himself he must prove he was a man. He had been so damned interested in proving he was a man that he had completely forgotten Doris.

"You know what I am?" he muttered. "I'm a letdown artist. I build it up and then I cut the rope and I let it fall down."

"Honey—"

"I let everything fall down."

"Listen, honey—"

"I'm no good."

"Sit down a minute. Listen to me—"

"What's the use? I'm just no goddamn good. I'm a bum. I'm a rumbum and a stumblebum and every kind of a bum. And that ain't all I am. I'm a cheap, low-down hypocrite."

Pauline had the bottle in her hand and she was pouring drinks. "You need something to pick you up."

"I need something to knock me down and bash my brains out."

He drank and she poured him another drink. And he drank that.

"I'm a hypocrite," he said. "And let me tell you something. There's nothing lower than a hypocrite."

"You need another drink. Here, take the bottle."

"Gimme the goddamn bottle." He tilted the bottle and took a very big drink. He put the bottle on the table. "Now let me tell you why I'm a hypocrite—"

"But you're not, you're not, you mustn't say that."

"I'll say it because I know it's true. I'm just a low-down

louse. And here's something else. You know why I'm getting kicked around? Because I deserve it. I'm getting exactly what I deserve."

He had the bottle again. He took a big drink and then held it up and looked at it. "Hello," he said.

Pauline stood up. "Now, for Christ's sake," she said. "Don't go crazy."

"I won't." He took another drink. "Maybe I'd be better off if I could. Because then I wouldn't know. At least it makes it easier when you don't know. When you're miles and miles away from yourself."

"Go on," she urged tenderly. "Take another drink."

"To get drunk? How could I get drunk? The way I feel tonight I could drink a gallon of it and not get drunk."

"Then take another nap," she said. "Go on, get in the cot and go back to sleep. That'll do you good."

He lifted the bottle once more. This time he kept drinking until he emptied it.

"It tastes like nothing at all," he said. "I can't even taste it."

"Go on, honey. See if you can go to sleep." She was shoving him gently toward the cot.

He fell on his back across the cot. Pauline lifted his legs and got his feet on the cot.

"Close your eyes," she said. "Take a nice long nap."

He closed his eyes. "Aviation," he mumbled.

"What? What, honey?"

"Aviation. I used to be in aviation."

"Sure. That's fine." She was backing across the room, toward the door. "Now go to sleep." She reached up and turned off the light.

"Aviator. Captain. Captain pilot, chief pilot. Captain bus driver. Make the trip with Captain Cassidy and we give you a guarantee. We give you a guarantee you won't come back alive. We're all proud of Captain J. Cassidy. He's the man at the wheel. There he is, the bastard, that's him—"

Pauline was at the door. She opened it and walked out. The door closed slowly and quietly.

"That's him," Cassidy mumbled. "I see him. His name is Jim Cassidy and he's trying to run but he ain't getting away. I see him now."

His head sagged down along the pillow. He groaned a few times. Then he was falling very swiftly toward sleep.

And as he fell, his lips moved. "Hey, listen. Listen, Mildred. I want to tell you something. No, nothing like that. Nothing rotten. I want to tell you something good. It's about you. I claim you're on the level. Now that's a compliment, you hear? Coming from me, that's a real compliment. You're on the level—"

He groaned again.

"What I gotta do is, I gotta think about this. About you, Mildred. I gotta think about you. Maybe I've had you figured all wrong. I don't know. I gotta think about it. Gotta—"

But then he was asleep.

Along then toward three in the morning he was awakened suddenly and roughly by a burst of loud laughter. It came from directly down below, from the back room where Lundy's special customers did their after-hour drinking.

The laughter reached a higher pitch. It was many voices laughing. Cassidy sat there in the darkness and listened to it and he climbed from the cot and inclined his head toward the floor to hear it more plainly. The laughing voices were fading one by one until there were only two laughing voices.

He recognized the laughing voices. He told himself he was wide awake and he wasn't imagining anything. They were down there together, Haney Kenrick and Mildred. They were sitting at a table together and having a fine time. Their shouts and shrieks of laughter became a blazing hot poker that sizzled into Cassidy's brain.

Chapter Fifteen

Immediately he wanted violence. He wanted to open the door and rush downstairs and smash their laughter down their throats. His hand went up and found the cord that switched on the light, and he took a few steps toward the door. Then it occurred to him that they weren't worth the trouble. Certainly they weren't worth the risk of having the police come in on it, and then the handcuffs and after that the cell bars. He started to focus on the practical side of the matter and he knew it involved the issue of ten, or twenty, or maybe even thirty years in prison.

The laughter was still coming up from downstairs but now he didn't hear it. He was moving toward the window. He opened the window very slowly and saw it had stopped raining. The air was warm and damp. He was leaning out and seeing the slanting roof just a few feet below the window. It was no problem to lower himself to the roof, then work his way down along the roof to the edge, then to dangle there for a moment, and drop to the alley behind Lundy's Place.

As he came down in the alley the loud laughter sounded very close. He turned and he was facing the window of the after-hours room. The window was partially open and he stood there listening to them and looking at them.

He told himself there was nothing to hear and nothing to see. If he used his head, he'd get away from this vicinity and do it fast. He'd aim toward the freight yards. Or maybe race to the docks and dive in and swim across to Camden. Then take it from there. Go anywhere. But he shouldn't hang around here. This area was poison, and the faces of his friends in Lundy's Place were the faces of grinning idiots. His dear, devoted friends were a morbid assemblage on an escalator slowly going down. They grinned at him, beckoned to him, and he heard the decay in their liquor-cracked voices. He started to move away from the window.

But somehow he couldn't keep moving away and he came back to the window and looked in. He saw them in there, in the room filled with smoke. They were there at their tables, some of them were leaning against walls, and one of them was asleep on the floor. Behind the cloudy curtain of cigarette smoke and liquor fumes their faces were gray and it seemed there was no light coming from their eyes.

And Cassidy realized that the laughter had faded, that the silence in the room was a heavy silence. Far back in his mind he could hear the echo of the laughter he had heard only moments ago, and then the echo faded also. He stood at the window and stared and saw Pauline and Spann gazing at each other and Pauline taking a cigarette from Spann's case. He saw Shealy and Doris lifting their glasses and offering a quiet, expressionless toast to nothing at all. He saw Mildred with her arms extended toward the table, her hands flat on the table, her fingertips gently tapping the table as Haney Kenrick sat there watching her and frowning and chewing on an unlit cigar.

Now he focused on Haney and he heard Haney saying, "What goes on here? What's the freeze all of a sudden?"

Nobody said anything.

"What's happened to the party?" Haney wanted to know. "Ain't we having ourselves a party?"

Mildred nodded. "Sure," she said. "We just need a refill, that's all."

Haney clapped his hands loudly. "By all means," he shouted. "A refill for the house."

Mildred looked at Lundy. "You hear what the man says? Drinks for everybody."

Haney smiled uncertainly. He glanced around the room, counting the faces. There were twenty-odd faces in the room and Haney took hold of Lundy's sleeve and said, "Now, wait—"

"Wait nothing," Mildred said. "The house drinks and it's on Haney." She stood up and everyone in the room was looking at her. "I'll order for the house. We'll all have whisky, Lundy. A bottle for each table."

"Well, now look," Haney said. "For Christ's sake—"

Cassidy watched it happening. He saw Lundy moving around with more speed and energy than usual. Then there was a fresh bottle on every table and Mildred was still standing and everyone was looking at her. Haney Kenrick was staring at her. Lundy stood at Haney's shoulder and Haney took out a roll of bills and paid for the drinks, his eyes darting from Mildred's face to the money and then back to Mildred's face.

Then Mildred lifted the bottle, lifting it slowly and as though she meant to drink from it. She tilted it slowly and then it was upside down and she was allowing the whisky to pour out and splash on the floor.

"What are you doing?" Haney demanded. Then he leaped up, because at all the other tables they were holding the bottles upside down and the whisky was pouring onto the floor.

"What is this?" Haney yelled.

They held the bottles upside down until all the whisky had drained out. The only customer who wasn't participating was Doris. She didn't understand what was happening, and her mouth was partly open as she watched Shealy shaking the bottle to make sure that the last drop of whisky would fall on the floor.

Haney's face was shiny and red. "Now, look," he said. "We've all been having fun tonight and I like a good time as well as anyone. But this goes too far. This ain't my idea of a joke."

Mildred turned slowly so that she was facing him. "It's my idea."

Haney swallowed hard. He opened his mouth to say something and shut it tightly and swallowed again. Finally he said, "I guess I'm stupid or something—"

"You?" Mildred murmured. She shook her head. "Not you, Haney. You're not stupid. You're a very smart engineer."

Haney put the cigar in his mouth, took it out and put it back in again.

Mildred said, "That's why you have money. That's why you wear good clothes. Because you got it up here," and she tapped the side of her head. "You're so much smarter than we are. You're so much better than we are. It's a cinch for you, isn't it?"

Haney took hold of the cigar and yanked it out of his mouth. "What's a cinch?"

"To put something over."

"On who? On you?" But his head was turning. He was looking at everyone.

Mildred said, "Look at me, Haney."

Haney pushed the cigar into his mouth. He looked at Mildred. He bit very hard on the cigar, as though he was trying to brace himself. "All right," he said, "I'm looking at you. Do I look worried?"

151

"No," Mildred said. "You don't look worried. You look scared stiff."

"Scared of what?"

"You tell us," Mildred said.

Haney sat down. He reached in his jacket pocket and took out some loose matches. He selected one, struck it on the sole of his shoe and began to light his cigar. The room was dead quiet while he lit the cigar. He puffed violently at the cigar and then he stood up and started toward the door leading to the outer room.

At the tables they were all quiet and they did not move. Haney was twisting his head in little darting movements as he approached the door. He put his hand on the doorknob. He turned the doorknob and started to open the doorway and realized nobody was going to stop him from making an exit. Now he was breathing hard and his face was turning from red to purple-red. The perspiration was dripping from his chin. His lips were trembling and couldn't support the cigar and he had to hold it in his hand. All at once he let out a string of very loud oaths and slammed the door shut and turned away from the door.

"You think I'm scared?" He put the question to all of them. "When a man is scared, he runs. You see me running?" He was moving across the room, walking from table to table. "I ain't running from anybody. I can look at each and every one of you. I can look you right in the eye. I can say to you I got a clear conscience."

Haney was at Spann's table when he said that, and Spann gazed meditatively at the center of the table.

It seemed that everyone was crowding Haney, although none of them had moved. He backed away from Spann's table, back toward the center of the room. "Now, listen," he said. "Listen carefully to what I have to say. If I didn't have a clear conscience, would I have come here tonight?"

Mildred left her table and moved toward Haney. She said, "You came here to sell us a bill of goods."

"Sell?" Haney widened his eyes. "What do you mean, sell? All night long I been sitting there telling jokes."

"And making us laugh," Mildred said. "Giving us a good

152

time. As if we're a roomful of feeble-minded animals. As if we got no brains, no feelings."

She came closer to Haney, and he began to back away from her.

She said, "You made a big mistake. You rated us people too cheap."

Then her arm was a cudgel, her hand was a fist banging him full on the mouth. She hit him again and he bent very low and let out a yowl. Mildred raised her arm to hit him again. She saw Shealy shaking his head, as though giving her some kind of a signal. Cassidy saw it from the window, and then it appeared that Mildred was accepting Shealy's advice. She turned away from Haney and went back to her table.

She sat down and lit herself a cigarette and leaned back to enjoy it. She was behaving as though nothing had happened. Haney took a long, grinding, very deep breath. He started toward Mildred, his arms outspread in a kind of pleading gesture. But then something seemed to occur to Haney and he whirled and aimed himself at the table where Shealy sat with Doris. Just at that moment Lundy was passing near the table and somehow Lundy got in Haney's path. There was a slight collision.

Haney grabbed Lundy and tossed him aside. Lundy fell against a table and tripped and went to the floor. Lundy yelped like a small animal and sat on the floor, and then his yelping was drowned in the thick growls that came from the other tables.

Cassidy saw the men rising slowly from their tables. He saw Spann smiling gently at the long blade that flicked in and out from its handle like the tongue of an anteater. He saw Haney turning to face the men and the naked terror in Haney's eyes.

Then Cassidy saw Shealy motioning to the men to sit down. In the same instant Haney had shot a glance at Shealy and saw the gesture and now, the terror was gone. It gave way to a thick-lipped grimace of bold challenge. Haney moved closer to Shealy and said, "Don't do me no favors. If they want to jump me, let them try it. There ain't a man here I can't handle." He heard himself sounding brave and it sounded very good to him. He looked at all the men and he said, "If anyone wants to try it, here I am. I ain't budging."

"Calm yourself," Shealy said. "This thing can be settled quietly."

Haney frowned. Without sound he was throwing questions at Shealy and without sound Shealy was answering the questions. Cassidy watched them as they held the silent conversation. It went on and on and gradually Cassidy's eyes moved across the table so that he wasn't looking at Haney and Shealy. He was looking at Doris and seeing the way she held the empty glass in her hand. Everyone else in the room was watching Haney but Doris was looking at her empty glass and waiting for someone to fill the glass. The only contact between Doris and the world was the glass. That fact, along with several other facts, was very clear to Cassidy as he stood there in the alley and looked through the window.

The moment of realization was almost tangible, like a page containing words of truth. Now he was able to understand the utter futility of his attempt to rescue Doris. There was no possibility of rescue. She didn't want to be rescued. His efforts to drag her away from the liquor had been based on a false premise, and his motive, now that he could see it objectively, had been more selfish than noble. His pity for Doris had been the reflection of pity that he felt for himself. His need for Doris had been the need to find something worth-while and gallant within himself.

He knew now that he had aimed his sentiment in the wrong direction. He had come close to handing Doris a raw deal. She was what she was, and she would never be anything else. She was perfectly and permanently married to her lover, the bottle.

The moment ended, and for Cassidy it meant the erasing of Doris. The next thing in his mind was the start of another discovery, but before he could concentrate on it, his attention was drawn to Haney Kenrick.

He saw Haney turning away from the table and moving in a completely confident, somewhat pompous fashion, toward the center of the room.

But now it was like a courtroom and there was something ceremonious in the way Shealy stood up, leaned across the table, pointed his finger at Haney and said, "You lied to the police. You can't lie to us."

Haney was jolted. He couldn't move. With his back to Shealy, he said, "I don't know what you mean."

"That's another lie."

The cigar was squeezed between Haney's teeth. He chewed heavily on it. He collected some more strength and arrogance and he said, "What makes you call me a liar?"

Mildred was standing again. "We know the truth."

"Yeah?" Haney managed a sneer. "Tell me all about it."

Mildred's fists were clenched again and she took a step toward Haney. But this time she was able to hold herself back. She said, "There's a phone over there," and she pointed across the room to a phone on the wall. "You see it, Haney?"

Haney stared at the phone. Then he looked at Mildred. Then again he stared at the phone.

"Here's what we want you to do," Mildred said. "We want you to go to the phone. Put a coin in."

As she spoke she was backing slowly toward the table where Pauline sat with Spann.

She said, "Put a coin in and call the police"

"What?" Haney mumbled. He was still staring at the phone. "What's that?"

"The police," Mildred said. Now she stood in front of Spann. Her right arm drifted backward so that Haney couldn't see what she was doing.

Cassidy stared and saw her fingers moving up and down and realized what she was doing. She was silently telling Spann to give her the knife.

And then Spann was sliding the switchblade into her palm, and her fingers closed on the handle.

"Call the police," Mildred said to Haney, "and tell them the truth."

Haney looked at her and grinned. It was a strangely twisted grin and there was a strange gleam in Haney's eyes. "You sound like you're begging me."

"All right," Mildred said. "I'm begging you to do it."

"That ain't the way I beg." Haney was breathing hard between his teeth. "You know the way I beg." He was breathing very hard and he made a hissing sound. He was looking at Mildred as though he were alone in the room with her. "When I beg, I get down on my knees. Remember, Mildred? Remember how I got down on my knees?"

Cassidy saw the way Mildred hefted the knife to get the feel of it as she held it behind her back. He gripped the sides of the window and told himself he ought to go in there now and take the knife away from Mildred.

"Let's see you do it," Haney said. "Let's see you get down on your knees and beg me." He let out a gurgling laugh. "Get down on your knees—"

"I would," Mildred said, "if I thought it would do any good."

Haney twisted the laugh and broke it off. "Nothing will do any good." He took a step toward her. "Now I'm finally doing it. I'm really giving it to you. Ain't I?" Just now he was slightly off-balance and his voice went up very high. "Now you're getting it good and proper and I'm really raining it into you."

Another laugh came rolling from Haney's lips, but then he choked on the laugh as Mildred moved her arm out in front and showed him the knife with the blade pointed at his stomach.

"I mean it," Mildred said. "You went and put my man on the hook. Now you get him off the hook or I kill you."

Haney Kenrick stood motionless and saw Mildred coming toward him with the knife. For an instant he was a frozen hulk of fright, but all at once he quivered and blazed and felt a blinding rage. The sum of it was too much. It was too much that Cassidy was all of Mildred's life and Haney Kenrick was just a big fat slob of blubber, a helpless target for the knife.

The rage burst wide open and Haney took an insane chance. He threw himself at Mildred, his arms sweeping downward. His hand closed on her wrist and twisted hard and the knife fell on the floor. Haney's other hand was a fist and he drew it back to his shoulder. He told himself he was going to smash her face. He was going to ruin the gorgeous face that he had worshiped. For a moment he tasted the pleasure of visualizing her ruined face.

At that moment Cassidy came crashing in through the opened window, came leaping and lunging, and hammered both hands to Haney's head. Haney staggered back and Cassidy hit him again, sent him to the floor, picked him up and knocked him down again. Haney tried to stay down and Cassidy put both arms around his throat and lifted him that way and dragged him across the room toward the phone on the wall.

Shealy was already at the phone, had inserted a coin, and was telling the operator to contact the police.

"No," Haney gurgled.

"No?" Cassidy tightened the hold on Haney's throat.

Haney gurgled again and managed to say, "All right."

Then Haney was on the phone. At the other end of the line a police sergeant told him to talk more clearly. It was very difficult for Haney to talk clearly. He was gagging and sobbing.

They had all left their tables and now they crowded around Haney and when it seemed that he couldn't stand on his feet they obligingly moved in to hold him upright at the phone. As Haney began to clarify his speech into the phone, Cassidy broke away from the group at the wall and looked for Mildred.

He saw her sitting alone at a table near the rear window. She had an arm hooked over the back of the chair and she was just sitting there and relaxing. Cassidy took the chair at the other side of the table.

"Where you staying?" he asked. He wasn't looking at her.

Mildred shrugged. "I came back to the flat." She was playing with a burned-out matchstick, using the blackened end to trace some kind of a design on the table. She said, "I'm sorry I threw your clothes in the river."

He wasn't looking at her. Something big and heavy was blocking his throat. He lowered his head to the side and bit very hard on his lip.

"What's the matter?" she said. "Hey, Cassidy, look at me. What is it?"

"It's all right." He swallowed the heaviness but still he wasn't able to look at her. "I'll be all right in a minute. Then I'll tell you what it is."

The End

BLACK LIZARD BOOKS